BEHOLD, THIS DREAMER

BEHOLD, THIS DREAMER

by

Robert E. Morrison

VANTAGE PRESS

New York   Washington   Atlanta   Hollywood

Volume II of the quintet: *The City of Light*

Volume I   *The Bird of Fire*
Volume II   *Behold, This Dreamer*
Volume III *Mary*
Volume IV   *Mums John*
Volume V   *The City of Light*

FIRST EDITION

Copyright © 1978 by Robert E. Morrison

Published by Vantage Press, Inc.
516 West 34th Street, New York, New York 10001

Manufactured in the United States of America
Standard Book Number 533-03796-4

Library of Congress Catalog Card No.: 78-057833

This book is dedicated to the millions of alcoholics in this land of forgotten dreams and to the memory of Edgar Allan Poe, who was murdered, as Baudelaire said; to the memory of Vincent Van Gogh, who was suicided by society, as Artaud said; to the memory of the immortal Dylan Thomas, who, not a little playfully, gave the booze a run for its money.

And, to my little brother Michael, who went to swap stories with them all over a fierce case of Johnny Walker Red.

"None of us are any longer material for a society."
Friedrich Nietzsche,
Joyful Wisdom

"We have exhausted nothing, you fool . . . *Seeing* is for impeccable men. Temper your spirit now, become a warrior, learn to *see* and then you'll know that there is no end to the new worlds for our vision."
Don Juan,
A Separate Reality

"A breath of our mouth becomes the portrait of the world, the type of our thoughts and feelings in the other's soul. On a bit of moving air depends everything human that men on earth have ever thought, willed, done and ever will do; . . ."

J. G. Herder,
Ideas on the Philosophy of the History of Man

"Language is the flower of the mouth. In language, the earth blossoms towards the bloom of the sky."
Martin Heidegger,
On the Way to Language

". . . With all our gentleness, patience, humanity and courteousness, we cannot persuade our nose to abandon its prejudice against the proximity of man . . ."
Friedrich Nietzsche,
Joyful Wisdom

"This shroud of night is not a mere darkening of the mind, no more than madness is dementedness. The night that shrouds the stranger's singing brother remains the 'ghostly night' of that death by which the departed died in the 'golden tremor' of earthliness."

Martin Heidegger,
On the Way to Language

"Who will sing us a song, a morning song, so sunny, so light and so fledged that it will not scare the tantrums—but rather will invite them to take part in the singing and dancing?"

Friedrich Nietzsche,
Joyful Wisdom

"How shall we sing the Lord's song in a strange land?"

Psalms: 137

"And it shall come to pass in the last days, saith God, I will pour out of my Spirit upon all flesh: and your sons and your daughters shall prophesy, and your young men shall see visions, and your old men shall dream dreams."

Acts 2:17,
The Holy Bible

"And when they saw him afar off, even before he came near unto them, they conspired against him to slay him.

And they said one to another, 'Behold, this dreamer cometh.'

Come now therefore, and let us slay him, and cast him into some pit and we shall say, 'Some evil beast hath devoured him'; and we shall see what will become of his dreams. . . .

And it came to pass when Joseph was come unto his brethren, that they stript Joseph out of his coat, his coat of many colors that was on him;

And they took him, and cast him into a pit; and the pit was empty, there was no water in it."

Genesis 18:21, 23-24,
The Holy Bible

BEHOLD, THIS DREAMER

Suggested background music for reading:

The Falconer's Arm,
Robbie Basho,
Volumes I and II

1

He had no teeth.
His gums were black with rot.
His stomach, a cesspool of bile.
His liver was shot.
And his pancreas swelled like a second heart in the middle of his chest, keeping him doubled over and vomiting throughout the day.
For the rest, he was dehydrated, kept alive by infrequent intravenous feedings of glucose, only

to return to the stations of his day, bowed in vomiting; bowed in shitting; bowed in drinking.

Yet no carbuncles had formed on his memory.

Strangely, they never would.

Shitmouth was his name when first I knew him and for long thereafter, a name that came to embody his breath and its sickening fragrance of rot and vomit, stale beer, and cheap wine sweetened by sorrow, fear, and the unrelenting smoldering of the purgatory that existence comes to be away from song and dream and good work. A fragrance somehow more metallic than organic, clouding his eyes with a yellowish gas.

Nor was his clothing less distinguished than his body. His rags seemed to have ejected on purpose from some shredding machine, to gather around and concentrate his odors in the boundaries of his presence. And because his bladder, too, had come upon its own independent course of action in his body, his clothing emanated the peculiar odor, known so well to the old, of a burst catheter.

And back when we first knew him, in the late fifties, while we were still quite young and hateful in the ghetto streets, his language was indeed the bloom of his mouth. In the two years of arid waste we spent at Saunsoci High School, before we dropped out and went our own, not altogether separate ways into wonder, we never heard him utter any other word than: "Shit!"

Johnny and I.

You'll remember Johnny.

Johnny Sceardi.

Mass-murderer Johnny.

Electrocuted at eighteen.

Justice done.

"Shit!"

That was all.

The single exclamation that gathered it all together in the framing of his presence among us, along the ghetto streets, before the passing eye, in the often turbulent but always secret systoles of our dreams.

But not before God.

No, there the matter was not settled.

The breath of his existence conspired with our youth and ignorance to evoke his name but not his being, his truth and lucidity; his strength and courage; his immense and truly golden quiet and gentleness.

No, we were too young to know of these things then, but I would learn in time. After Johnny was gone.

And, in time, I would seek out his true name. But Shitmouth is how it began with us, and that is how it must remain for a while.

II

He had found something of a cloistered place to
shelter him from wind and sight, a crevice between
two gray stone walls of the school buildings on
the gravel grounds of Saunsoci High. Here he
dwelt with the furniture of his habits; two rusted
coffee cans, one for vomiting, the other should his
bowels take him unawares; rumpled newspaper;
and, incongruously, a many-colored quilt, always
clean and radiant amid the destitution, filth, and
ravagement.

How long he had lived in the crevice, I do not know. The two years I was at the school and after, until one night, not too long ago, the students, black and white together, burned the place to the ground, and he was trapped in there, too drunk to move or perhaps unwilling.

His ashes settled in a pile between the blackened walls. Scarcely a pocketful.

After the authorities had left the scene, and I was able to reach the crevice, I came upon the ashes there and the melted coffee cans.

And laughter.

Full-throated laughter was stirring in the ashes, defining their boundary, rising nearly to the strength of song in my ears and then subsiding. And silence.

I sat through the night, and when morning came, gathered the ashes in the sun and brought them home and gave them to the whore Mary Hynes.

And she took them to a home more distant than I could, a place of light and warmth and safety; a place of love.

Now, she, too, is dead.

And Johnny with many others.

While I sit, waiting for the courage to follow them all.

III

In those earlier days, I did not know his age or his place of origin. This latter, some vast and altogether lonely place I had supposed. Someplace where the motions of a man are rooted in the wind, possibly not of this land.

But his age seemed to issue from the individual moments guarded by the circumstances of our encounters. There were moments when his laughter sprayed our conversation with the effervescence of a child's heart, and I thought he was younger than man. But these were not too often and did little more than stir a sorrow and loneliness in me; the wish to have known him before booze became the medium of his passage among us.

On other occasions, I sat apart and studied him in the bar as he fought back tears, swelling in rhythm with the songs rising from the juke box, and talked with Mary Hynes; tears, which were the finest compliment he had left to give the women he had known, secured, and lost. At these times, the furrows of his face widened to the edge of his presence, and the clouded yellow of his skin and eyes lifted, seemed to escape the room as though it were sucked forward into a future that had by error come too soon. Then I had thought he was young, not more than thirty, yet to spend his passions gathering flowers.

Too, there were those moments when I had grown older, and I sought him out to explain some paradox, to answer some riddle of thought or just relieve a nameless anxiety that plagued me. Then I found him older, late in his forties or early in his fifties, such the depth of his perception and understanding, such the exquisite richness of his memory. There, bent in our intensities, I did not notice the weight of his breath, only the utter freedom of his words, which shone like polished stones. Something the immortal Dylan said, himself not far from the crevice, something about "the pebbles of the holy streams."

And there were always times, as when I first saw him years ago, that I saw what others saw, a broken blotch of a man shuttling through the ghetto streets, bent sideways away from things and down toward rest; times when I thought he must be seventy or eighty and soon to pass over.

7

As well, those long quiet moments that came
to haunt my memory, and, in their haunting, to
spawn a rendevous and a rapprochement between
my hatred of man and my love of nature. Those
long quiet moments as I watched him sleeping
in the crevice, guarded by his stupor, when my
thought reached out to vaguely touch the infinite
and I felt that he did not exist at all. But that was
after I began to see the blueness that seemed to
enshroud him as he slept; the blueness of mountain
twilight, the seed ground of vision.

All to few were those watchings.

And not a little saddened by the things that
we had done to him in the frenzy of our ignorance
and the hatefulness with which we prowled the
streets, retaliating for the rape that had already
been perpetrated on the dreams of this land and
spawned the bastard child everyone called reality.

Things that we had done to him, Johnny and I:

As on the cold and snowing winter night when
we found him sleeping in the crevice, covered by
his many colored quilt, truly a Joseph's coat, I came
to understand, a gift from a far place to keep him
warm as he wandered in this alien and inhuman
land.

We snatched the quilt off him, kicking him
awake with old wino jeers and taunts, and then we
ran laughing through the bursting flakes to a corner
of the school yard where we burned it to warm
our hands. But the fire was strange, dark blue in the
center, white in the flame, yielding neither heat nor
ash. The quilt more evaporated than burned as Shitmouth crawled toward us, screaming: "Shit! Shit!
Shit!"

The fire frightened us, and we ran; ran when

we should have stayed, for had we stopped and wondered, it is possible that there is much that would not have happned. Johnny was the first to know. That night he had a dream, and when I saw him the next day, he was deep in his moods.

I said: "Johnny, what the hell are you so depressed about?"

He more whispered than spoke.

He said: "Shitmouth's quilt was made in the City of Light."

"Bullshit, Johnny. He's just a stinking old wino. He couldn't see the City if he was staring at it."

And I laughed and chided him about his dream, for there was much that I did not know and much about the City, so dear to Johnny's dreams, that I could neither fathom nor trust. And though there is much that I still do not know, my distrust would vanish one day, and I would move the earth to see and touch that quilt again and beg all of life for a key to the City. Which may yet be given me, as it was given to Johnny and his father, Big Sam Sceardi. As it was given to Shitmouth and Mary Hynes and many others, who suffered more than I from the profanation of all that is holy.

Shitmouth never got another quilt.

From that night on, he slept only in the rags he wore, protected by the blueness that I was eventually to see.

Meanwhile, Johnny capped his dream, and we made terror for Shitmouth whenever we could.

If we found him in the daylight, sleeping in the sun against some fence or tree, we would kick him awake and run in gales of hollow laughter hounded by his single scream: "Shit!"

9

And if we came upon him in the crevice, and he was drunk enough, we rolled him for whatever change he had.

In those early days, we thought Shitmouth made his money selling booze to the kids in school; certainly he had bought beer for us a number of times for the price of a shot or so. And business would have been brisk, for few thought of suffering through classes without being loaded or having a pint close at hand to stave off the bombardment of trivia, just as now, in our own time, few think of going to those same classes without being stoned on weed or speed, acid or coke, smack or skag, as they came to say and bought in that same crevice where others came to ply their wares. Not a few times did we have to postpone our assaults when Shitmouth was surrounded by students, laughing, drinking, and talking, sometimes, however, simply meditating in silence. We took these gatherings for parties and the students for upperclassmen at Saunsoci High because they looked older, and some wore suits and ties, but then, in those days, everybody looked older to me, and I thought little of it. Now I have only the memory of those gatherings and a hunger to have been a part of them.

But the law intervened the last time we rolled him. It was nearing three in the morning, and Johnny found a medallion in his pocket with about seven dollars and change. He took the medallion, and I took the change.

Shitmouth sat up abruptly.

There was such an intense lucidity in his eyes, it was impossible to imagine he was drunk.

He said nothing.

10

He locked Johnny's eyes into that incredible stare and sucked the reality out of him. Johnny began to tremble and fold. Then, slowly, almost imperceptibly, he handed the medallion back to Shitmouth.

But I kept the change and walked away.

When Johnny caught up with me, I said: "Johnny, what the hell did you do that for? We could have pawned it."

He said: "Give me the money!"

He was still trembling, and his voice had no foundation.

I said: "Here's your half."

He turned in a trance and returned to Shitmouth. Handed over his half of the money.

I could hear vague murmuring as they talked, and I remember feeling alarmed at the thought that Shitmouth could utter more than a single word.

I called to Johnny, and he came away deep in his moods again.

Later, he said: "We will never touch Shitmouth again."

"Why?"

"The medal was made in the City of Light."

"How do you know?"

"The Law was written on it."

Johnny had taught me the poets law, burning on the mountain, which protected the entrance to the City of Light, as he had learned it from his father: *"Each shall guard the other's solitude."*

I was stunned.

I said: "Johnny, where do you suppose he got it?"

"I don't know. Maybe he's been there."

"But the times that you were there and all the times your father has been there, did either of you ever see him?"

"No. I never saw anybody. I don't know about dad."

I said: "Maybe he stole it."

Johnny laughed. His certainty had returned. He said: "Nobody ever steals anything from the City of Light."

The episode disturbed me deeply, and we never did touch Shitmouth again, nor do I remember what impulse made me hide the money away and never use it until the night that Johnny died.

For he went on to kill many and die in the electric chair.

The night they threw the switch, I took the money and bought a pint of whiskey and went to the crevice, surprised to see Mary Hynes sitting there with Shitmouth. They fell silent as I approached. I sat down. Handed him the change that was left. Opened the bottle and passed it.

I remember thinking that Mary Hynes, whose beauty had been famous in the streets when first I had encountered her, was near death herself, so bruised and bloated had she become.

Shortly before midnight, Mary lit a candle, and Shitmouth took out his medallion and placed it in the light. As with the quilt, the light from the burning candle was blue in the center and white in the flame, but this time it did not frighten me, and I saw a city and mountain etched into the gold and the words: "*Each shall guard the other's solitude.*"

At midnight, the two of them joined hands

over the medallion, but when I reached to touch it, they said: "No! Not you."

Then he opened his mouth and screamed: "Shit!"

And Mary wept silently, knowing that this existence could not contain the dreams of men and that she and Shitmouth must follow Johnny soon.

The candle evaporated as the quilt had done, and Shitmouth returned the medallion to his pocket.

I remember thinking: *Johnny is safe now. He's gone home.*

And though Saunsoci was a blur of sirens, I could not imagine that Big Sam Sceardi, Johnny's father, had broken out of the asylum and shot Johnny's mother and himself, even as the candle flamed and we sat in the crevice.

In that moment, I became homeless, for since, my mother died and my father soon after I had lived with Margaret Sceardi and Candy, Johnny's sister.

Now there was nothing. Neither friend nor home nor access to the City of Light, and I set my face against the reality that had darkened so many of my days and slowly began to learn, until one day Shitmouth did most certainly let me hold the medallion, and I have it now before me because Mary gave it to me when I brought it to her with his ashes.

But the key to the City of Light?

No. I still do not have the key.

And Mary, too, is gone.

IV

This moment, as I sit holding the medallion, I know the City exists, for I have seen it. Seen it not always drugged but in the clear light of dawn as well. Seen it strung between two mountain peaks, with the law inscribed in fire on the mountain side. A place of beauty and grace; a place of freedom, safety, and solitude, overwhelming in its simple radiance.

Yet even after all that has happened, I am still uneasy, for I fear the romanticism that drives men to abandon themselves and their deepest energy and thus prepares the ground for tyranny. And I fear as much the structure and content of utopias, which can not compel the cynic to celebrate the light as his own nature and being, the vicious finitude of men that sours the dreams of life, curdling them into ideology. And because I can not always see, perhaps what I fear the most is the enormous waste of time and creativity that would have occurred should the City be but an illusion; should it be not the flower of primordial energy but the dark bloom of energy gone to seed in the unholy night of reality. Perhaps it is my own weakness that I fear, that, like Judas, I yet want much of the strength of suicide to go beyond and be certain that all that has happened and all that has been seen was not illusion.

And yet I know the City exists; that strong men and women have seen it, and some have gone there, and many more intend the trip.

It was Big Sam Sceardi who first brought us concrete news of the City, though Johnny seemed to have known of it from the beginning. Big Sam found it on Iwo and Tarawa in the midst of war and killing and the stench of death unremitting. There he turned from the careless, jocular, and fleeting apprehension of things and men. Drawing a veil over his sun, he turned into darkness and the awesome abyss that men who matter scurry to avoid, measuring their success in the degrees by which they remove themselves from the precipice and block the path to it with odd and sundry but always finite edifices. This, even though the abyss lay directly behind their eyes and, unconquered, haunts their every move, their every love and embodiment, until, in weariness, it sallies to the fore, demanding its own accounting, gathering up the edifices and trucking them off to the ever-smoldering fires of waste, ringing the song of death.

With Big Sam it was different:

When he returned from the war to Margaret and Johnny and Johnny's brother Frank, Candy was conceived, and Big Sam abandoned them all and took himself into the dark, fetid alleys of the ghetto, consigning himself and all he saw to the hell of existence until, but an instant from suicide, he found a ruler for his City, a dark-haired goddess of incomparable beauty and grace whom he took to be creation but whom Johnny, working his own way through that same abyss, took to be the goddess of death; an ambiguity that the ancients may have resolved with the tree of life; with Isis; or the essential episodes that gave Eve her name.

It was only then that Big Sam belched out of the dark with tales of the Light and astounded the authorities with the information that he would work and support his family only in his City. So adamant did he become on this point, so compelling his conviction, that he stirred the ghost behind their eyes, and they filed papers and cuffed him off to his allotted bed in the asylum. The bed that waits for all who think to dream the primordial dream among the traitors in this too tyrannous land. This land itself, conceived in the dreams of those who broke the shackles of older tyrannies and escaped from a hundred lands, dreams not too long in the eye before they were stretched and mutilated on the racks we call our schools, unholy dungeons of the Apocalypse yet coming.

16

Is it not always the hideous schools that castrate and mutilate a people, prepare them for slavery?

Has it not always been so?

Is it not so now?

I know I but barely escaped it when I dropped out and set my face against reality. But maybe not soon enough. Maybe all my fears about the City stem from having stayed too long. Perhaps that fear is the festering disease of an abortion commenced but interrupted.

But Johnny seemed to escape altogether when, like Big Sam, under the shroud of darkness, he found the City and the Light and with his girl friend Tarinia, prepared the plans to hasten there and conceive in freedom.

And so, apart from the Law and the structure of the place, there is not much I can relate of its workings; the patterns of its governance and the role of the dark-haired goddess; the daily comings and goings of its people; the larger orbits of what it holds holy and within its power to accomplish and sustain. A few things I learned from Big Sam; a few from Johnny, Shitmouth, and Mary, and these I can record in their place. But until I learn to trust, to come more fully into the light, much will remain unknown to me. For now it is enough to see that the thing exists, that men and women have found their way to it, while others are on the path, and still greater numbers cock their ears and strain toward rumors in the streets, rumors of an exodous coming, so vast as to be unparalleled in the existence of man.

V

After that night in the crevice, the night that Johnny was murdered and all my homes were gone, it was several months before I encountered Shit-mouth again.

I had yet another rendezvous with the hateful contingencies of existence.

Candy and I could no longer live in the house Big Sam had built before the war and to which they returned after he burst from darkness, the place having been rented during that time, as the family moved to the ghetto to be near him should he need them. As they had done with my father's house, the morticians, in league with the cemetery directors and whatever other authorities such thefts require, stole the house and land for their services and sold it.

Candy and I pawned what little there was to pawn, and she at fifteen and I at nineteen went our separate ways into the ghetto streets. Candy with her guitar and her songs reaching into the soul of woman and I with my pen and the first act of my play about the wind, the Saunsoci Play House production of my play about the sun already fallen into oblivion, not to be seen again until many more died and then in alien cities.

What change I had was soon gone, and I found myself in those same alleys, among the foul garbage where Big Sam had dwelt so long.

Thin, scarcely over a hundred pounds on a six-foot stack of bones, it was not long before my stomach gnawed into its lining. But after a week, the sour acid went away, allowing a kind of euphoric numbness to set in. I could do no more than manage an enfeebled wave to check the bold assaults of the rats. Then, to be sure, the vicious rains came, cold, torrential, mocking, and with them, paranoia on a grand scale; paranoia intensified by the winos trying to roll me from time to time and kicking me when they found no change; paranoia that infested every movement that I contemplated until my mind had the character of the rats watching over me.

So it was on the seventh day of the rains that

the poet Stephen, his daughter Deirdre on one shoulder a crate of grapefruit ripped from some supermarket on the other, thundered down the alley.

In my feverish delirium, it was the silence of the rats, the cessation of their interminable chirping, that I noticed first, and I thought I had surely died, and they had made done with me. Then I felt Stephen nudging me with his toe, and when my face reorganized, and I was able to force my eyes open, I saw him standing there, six foot four with streams of water splashing from his long blond beard, a Neptune rising from the sea, or possibly Balder the Beautiful.

He said: "What are you into, brother?"

My mouth fumbled with itself, and I could not answer.

He said, "Well, there's a mattress in the corner and stew in the pot." And he strode off as I fought so desperately to rise, to gather together all the disjoined parts of what was left of my body that would not or could not function as a whole.

It seemed that all of life turned over before he stopped, retraced his steps, and saw I could not move.

He lowered the crate of grapefruit gently, camouflaged it with garbage cans. Then he scooped me up in one arm, throwing me over his shoulder in a single motion, and set off with the two of us, Deirdre and I, saddled in the rhythm of his motions.

And so it was by a tortuous route that I came to live in the tenement where Johnny lived with his mother and brother and Candy while Big Sam was gone; in the tenement where Mary lived and

20

the old cowboy Mums John, who never spoke, and Stephen the poet.

Grapefruit juice and tea and toast quelled my fever in a week or so and inhibited the constant shaking, and my eyes returned, and I could see again the deeper outlines of things.

Deirdre, at first, her dreamy face in front of mine, forcing me to drink, then the sounds of Stephen reaching from across the room, and, finally, Stephen himself bent over his typewriter, pounding furiously, tearing out pages, balling them up, hurling them with all his strength at the opposite wall, Frenzy followed by exhaustion. Gradually, the room itself with gaping holes in the plaster, their mattress, a chair and table, an orange crate with a hot plate on top. The toilet, I knew from when I use to come here, was down the hall.

And then the odors came, the sickening smell of dead things in the place that kept me vomiting for days before I found my speech.

I said: "What the fuck is that smell?"

Stephen halted in the midst of his barging and plunging motions at the typewriter.

"Rats!" he yelled. "Fuckin' a rats!"

Then I saw them scattered around the room in traps, all dead; the skeleton beginning to show through some.

Stephen stormed across the room to my mattress.

He said: "So you're back among the living. Welcome home, brother. Deirdre, get him something solid to eat!"

I said: "That smell. I'd just puke it."

"Yeah, well look on the bright side. The fucking dead ones keep the live one away. Rats don't like to be around their dead any more than humans do."

He paused, staring at the corpses, eyes blank with hatred. "Bastards just about killed Deirdre one night," he mumbled, turning to me. "You'll get use to the smell in a little while. Concentrate on the fruit."

"The fruit?"

"Yeah, the dump is loaded with rotting fruit. Can't you smell it?"

"No."

"Concentrate!"

I did and detected a vague whiff of overripe fruit, sweet in the hollow of the animal death.

"Got it?"

"Yeah."

"Well, just remember that it's there and continue to concentrate on it. You set one pile of shit against another, and pretty soon you got a whole new thing, like mixing paints. Simple dialectics."

Then he laughed, returning to his typewriter, and Deirdre brought me a plate of cold tuna with lemon.

But it didn't stay down.

Not that day.

Nor for several after until I mastered the form and content of the dialectic and resigned myself to the knowledge that ultimately you can live with anything.

But why?

What rottenness is bred so deep into the soul of our people that the finest and the best of its possible culture must be brought forth in filth, squalor, and contingency too vast for the human mind to endure. That those charged with its creation, men who should bring tidings from the sea, the clean mountains, and the preparate earth, must drag the holy and varied muses through shit and death and become so paranoid in the execution of their sacred trust, the protection of these holy ones, that they rent their love asunder and become as surly and hatefully petty as the roaches and the rats are quick.

What rottenness is bred so deep in our people that like the jackal it consumes its own entrails and with a mouth of shit turns to breathe on its father's dreams.

No curiously sensuous Bohemia this; this place of rot, vermin, and violence, of incredible waste and ignorance and unending terror.

Masochistic beyond belief, do you not come in droves to pretty places to see and marvel at what grew in the shit, and do you not rejoice over the absence of any human visage there, even as the immortal prophet of Sils Marie, the son of the morning, thunders from his grave the damnation of all this lostness.

Why sustain this terror?

The Muses know.

They know that although it be ripped asunder and fouled with madness, the love of the artist is stronger than death and the rottenness that surrounds him; stronger than time and all its petty ways; as strong as God.

But do not feel content in that, for his hate is equally strong. Strong enough to destroy you, to remove the filth of your existence from the memory of man and for generations if need be; strong enough to set the face of history against your finiteness so that only your shame remains, and you will pray fiercely for a finer, more noble aspect to your sojourn.

And am I not angry?

I surely am!

I surely am!

And not a little because of Shitmouth.

VI

When I did see him again, it was at Harry's Bar
and Grill, a few doors down from our tenement.
I was sipping a beer at the bar when I saw him,
framed in the greasy light, sitting at a precariously
broken three-legged table by the juke box, which
blurted alternately Sinatra and Bennett and that
tinny country Western that was spawned on the
outskirts of neon all across the land. His glass was
empty in his hands; eggshells scattered around him;
an abstract grin on his face; his eyes not particularly

glazed, his gaze off in some other part of the world.

The place breathed the odors of old wood soaked in stale beer, mingled with urine and clouded over with a syrupy disinfectant that fought with the hamburger grease always trying to escape from the kitchen. Later, toward evening, the grease would win, and the disinfectant would go into hiding until closing time. Nor was the befouling of the air lessened by the smell of the winos themselves as they sat scattered around the room, alone in booths, at tables, sometimes folded up on the floor by the urinal. Harry would not let them sit or stand at the bar because of their stench, which he felt drove the other regular customers away. Indeed, I heard that he had once barred Shitmouth altogether until he had diluted the odor of his presence, which was strong enough to keep the police at bay. So badly did he contaminate their clothes and cars that they avoided him as cautiously as a hunter avoids an encounter with a skunk. But Mary, whose peculiar relationship with Harry gave her a certain authority in the place, had interceded, and Shitmouth could usually be found at the table by the juke box when he wasn't at the crevice.

This afternoon, Mary was not there.

Hardhats were busy at the bar, their clothes and faces caked white with lime.

Quaffing drafts.

Generating hollow loudness, profuse with profanity; "shit," "fuck," and "motherfuck" running in torrents from their mouths, to sweep into oblivion this or that particle of inane information forgotten before it was proffered and followed by a flurry of "us-and-them" backslapping and shoulder punching and queer little witticisms, grinning out the image of this or that cunt, always fucked in strange places, the invariable and unvarying glue of the uneasy camaraderie of such as these, whom some call the salt of the earth.

"Hey, Harry!" one of them yelled. "Matcha for the box."

Harry, red-faced and paunchy, nearly bald, waddled from the kitchen in his grimy apron. Took fifty cents from the cash register. Flipped it. Failed to match. Frowned. Waddled back to the kitchen, the entire transaction counted in seconds but powerful enough to occur in dead silence, shored up by the muscled tension peculiar to the gambled moment and released in a flood of "you-lucky-son-of-a-bitch-you" commentary, each having weighed their own chances against the spinning coins.

"Play the Red Foley one!" one of them yelled as the winner detached himself from the group and headed for the box.

What happened next was too sudden to comprehend.

I heard someone shouting behind me: "Well, whatta ya gotta say, huh? What the fuck ya gotta say, anyhow!?"

As I turned, I saw the hardhat step back from the box, raise his arm, and throw his glass as hard as he could at Shitmouth's face.

The glass froze in the air like the fabled arrow of Parmenides, and I saw Shitmouth grinning, then the glass again, then blood spurting from his forehead.

Utter shock.

My eyes lost their focus.

A thin, warm stream of urine coursed down my leg and chilled.

Unconsciously, I slid off the stool and started to the back of the room. Hardhat hands grabbed me by the shoulder, spun me around, flung me at the wall: "Wheredafuckyathink you're goin', punk?"

I slid to the floor and puked.

Harry emerged from the kitchen, gripping a sawed-off shotgun.

He said: "All right boys, get on outta here and don't come back till you cool off."

They regrouped.

Tried to stare the gun out of Harry's hands.

Looked vacantly at each other.

Said: "Fuckin' winos."

Put a cool image on their departure; sauntered out the door.

Harry peered around the corner, looked at Shitmouth, then at me. Returned to the kitchen shaking his head.

I pulled myself to the bar on the backs of chairs, found a bar rag and lurched over to Shitmouth.

He was bent over holding his head in his shaking hands.

The blood spurting between his fingers formed a pool on the floor in which floated shattered glass and eggshell. Though dried into the wood, the pool of blood is still there by the corner of the juke box today, and though I have often thought of marking it off as a holy spot, I haven't yet.

Prying his hands away, I could see that the gash, directly over his left eye, was acutely deep, and there were bits of glass embedded in it.

Shitmouth went limp in my arms when I pressed the rag into a compress over the wound, and as I held him up and moved him toward the door, I remember a sense of amazement at how utterly light and frail he was.

"Harry!" I shouted. "Give me a hand getting him to Stephen's."

Not a sound from the kitchen.

Shitmouth was not completely out.

He tried to get his feet under him.

Stumbled around in my arms.

Holding the compress with one hand, I managed to get him to the front and out.

Harry stood expressionless at the entrance to the kitchen.

Stephen was asleep when we struggled into the room.

Deirdre gone to school.

Settling Shitmouth into the chair at the typewriter, the only chair in the room, it took me several minutes to rouse Stephen.

When he woke, he looked at me blankly. Than at Shitmouth. He winced perceptibly when he saw him. Jumped naked from the bed. Dashed to the typewriter and yanked it out from under Shitmouth, who had slumped over it the instant I had left his side.

The keys were coated with blood.

"For Christ's sake," he shouted, "get the blood off this thing before it hardens and fucks everything up!"

He pitched it into my arms and pulled Shitmouth's head back over the chair in the same motion.

Gently, he lifted the compress, forcing the head into the light.

"Fuckin' glass in there," he muttered. "Shakey, get me the first-aid kit."

"Where?"

"Behind my mattress! Hurry up! What the hell are you doing standing around with the typewriter. Give me the kit, and get that thing cleaned while I work on this."

I found a knapsack full of bandages and implements behind the mattress where he and Deirdre slept.

Calmly, the naked doctor worked.

He tweezed out the bits of glass until he was satisfied there were none left, then bathed the wound in some solution, which must have burned like hell, gauging from the frantic twitching of Shitmouth's legs. But it stopped the bleeding.

I said: "It sure looks like it needs a batch of stitches."

"Stitches cost money," Stephen mumbled. "He'll just have another scar. We'll put a butterfly on it."

He squeezed the wound closed and laced it over with Scotch tape. Over that, he pressed a large Band-Aid.

I said: "Do you think he got a concussion?"

With a flashlight, he peered into Shitmouth's eyes. "No way to tell without X rays."

He patted Shitmouth on the shoulder. "It'll be all right, brother," he said. "In a few days, your eyes will swell up and turn black and blue, but don't worry about it. It's just the old lymph doing its work. You want something to eat? There's stew in the pot."

Shitmouth waved the question aside and stared at Stephen, who did not move but simply stared back.

I had the uncanny sensation of some communication taking place that excluded me.

Then the tears flowed down Shitmouth's face, dribbled on to Stephen's hands, holding Shitmouth's face; quiet, immense tears of error and incomprehension; tears of the child forever wronged.

When he did move, Stephen said simply: "Peace, brother, peace. There will be time." And he turned away to stare out the window.

Shitmouth stood up.

Gathered himself toward the door.

Left, saying nothing.

At the window, I felt Stephen's presence as I had not known it in his barging at the world. The presence of some vast sorrow that gathered its certainty from high places and deep winds, a sorrow blockaded by time until it exploded and became the face of life.

He stood there heavily silent for a few moments and then raised his fist and shook it at the street.

An agonizing scream tore from his mouth.

A scream without words that stopped my ears with terror; a cut gut scream that had already howled in the corridors of my heart, as I had heard it from Mary, Johnny, Margaret Sceardi, and many others before I set it loose in my own throat, and black murder rose in my eyes, requiring utter genocide for its satisfaction, for its rest.

When it subsided, and he sat at the typewriter, staring at the door, I said: "Stephen, do you know Shitmouth?"

He said: "Yeah, I've seen him around."

But, again, I noticed that he winced perceptibly, and I sensed something strange in his manner.

But I did not pursue it then.

I said: "You sure did a good job on his head."

He said nothing.

Got up.

Went back to bed.

While my own head slipped out to mingle with the broken, humbled street, gathering the fragments of a thousand fleeting impressions from all my growing there. The crowing rooster that was my memory, prepared to mount the pecking hen of my sight, and from that not altogether sane, all too depressing fuck, an egg would issue, which, when brooded upon, would surely crack, and the fledgling image of Shitmouth would come to dwell overtly in the house of my heart.

Never to be forgotten.

From that moment, to be nurtured with wonder, to grow beyond memory, to become history and, perhaps, the shame of all reality.

How long?

How long from encounter to memory? And from there to history?

Not long.

From encounter to memory, no longer than a man's nap.

From memory to history, no longer than the growth of the fledgling image into the reality from which it itself had come.

I resolved in the twilight of the room to investigate remorselessly the silent tears of a man gone to rot and find the secret of their immensity.

VII

When Stephen woke, he jolted me from my reverie, and the street returned to itself, no longer dependent on my sight and memory.

He said: "Shakey, what are your plans?"

His eyes were flat.

His voice without color.

There was a large tension in the room that I could not immediately comprehend, and my stomach quickened with the thought that I had stayed too long and was about to lose yet another home.

And my face was full of alleys.

I said: "Plans?"

"Yeah, plans. You figure to crash here permanently, or you figure to get a job and hit it on your own?"

He was sitting naked on the edge of the mattress, his head resting on his knees, turned toward me.

I could not meet his eyes.

Tried to focus on his beard while I searched my memory for information that if properly used, would secure my mattress.

I knew that Stephen was a poet who could sell nothing of what he wrote.

I knew that he had dropped out of the University in his sophomore year for the same reasons I had dropped out of high school in the tenth grade, to study and do his own work, being constantly assaulted by the vicious impotence of morbidly trivial faculty.

I knew he didn't work. That he collected enough from ADC (Aid to Dependent Children) for the rent and generally managed to steal enough food in the city to keep himself and Deirdre healthy.

Deirdre!

Was she the key?

She was there, though I had not seen or heard her enter. She was standing by the hot plate against the wall, glancing worriedly from one to the other of us, holding the bloody rag from Shitmouth's wound.

She said: "Shakey can stay with us, can't he, daddy?"

Stephen didn't answer her; shifted his head, bringing my eyes into line.

34

I said: "Plans?" The question far too feeble in its repetition and not a little ringed with fright.

"Yeah. You know. Plans."

And did I not think for just a second that I could get out of the stench of dead rats and rotting fruit, the unholy alliance between sight and smell, and go off to a beautiful place and there prevail.

I did.

For a second, I did. But that is all. Experience had long since taught me that all the beautiful places were under guard and chained.

I said: "I can't get a job, Stephen. You know I don't have a diploma or anything. I want to finish my play about the wind."

He fumbled around in a stack of papers by his mattress. Found the oilcloth folder I kept it in.

"This?" he asked, thumbing through it.

"Yeah."

"I read it when you were still out with the fever."

I waited as he stroked his beard absently, and his eyes roamed around me, making me feel terribly small and inconsequential.

Finally, he said: "You're having trouble with it. Hung up on the breeze, near as I can see."

He was right, of course. The play was to begin with utter silence, lasting one act, just as my play about the sun had begun with darkness. Then it was to progress from the breath of a bird's warble to the faint touch of air, building to a cyclone, and then to silence again, without the presence of a single human. Yet another dialectic. But there was something about the sensuous plenitude of the breeze that so far had eluded me.

I said: "I may be too young for the breeze."

"Or too morbid."

"Yeah."

He said: "I saw your play about the sun. I didn't think it was possible to write a play without people."

"Why not? You write poetry without words. Besides, there was a naked woman in the end of the sun play, but they said it was obscene and cut it out."

"I thought something was missing."

He fell silent for a moment.

"Can't you get some bread for the sun to see you through the wind?"

"No. They all went away with long faces."

He stood up then.

Went to the window, his hands clasped behind him, making motions as though he were working worry beads.

The room was dark now.

Deirdre came and stood by him, her right hand gentle on his elbow.

Together they watched the neon mock the departing twilight and wrestle its way into the darkness and throw and pin it on the mat of human waste.

I thought I heard him whisper: "There must be a better way."

Then he turned, his naked form outlined against the garish glow of the street. Looked at my mattress; at Deirdre; finally, at me.

He said: "Yeah, well, all right. You can stay here, but there is one rule. I don't want anybody around me when I'm working. Agreed?"

"Agreed."

The tension drained out of me.

My body expanded in a smile.

Deirdre said: "I'm glad."

Kissed her father.

Then me before she lit candles in the room.

I said: "I have another plan, too."

"Yeah?" he said, pulling on his trousers.

"I'm going to find out about Shitmouth. I was thinking while you were sleeping that he might be able to teach me something about the breeze."

His face flared with anger.

"Don't call him that!"

"What, Shitmouth?"

"Yeah."

"Why?"

"Just don't call him that around me. It's not his name, and it burns my balls."

"So you do know him?"

"I knew him, and you can do me a favor by not bringing him here again."

"Why? Who is he? What's his name?"

"I don't want to talk about it."

He turned away from me, but not before I saw a darkening anguish in his eyes and thought it best to let it drop for the moment.

It was a preview of all the troubles I was to have trying to find out about Shitmouth.

Deirdre ladled out three bowls of stew, and we ate in silence, but I could feel an immense depression rising in Stephen.

He threw his empty bowl on the floor and jerked open the door, snuffing out the candles.

In the darkness, he turned, barely outlined against the hall light. He said: "Just don't bring him here anymore."

I said: "What the hell is his name?" I've always called him Shitmouth. What am I suppose to call him?"

There was a long pause.

"Tanner. His fucking name is Tanner. Mr. Robert T. Tanner."

"Yeah, well who the hell is he?"

Just before he slammed the door, he said: "Ask Mary."

I asked Deirdre.

She said: "Daddy doesn't talk about him." With that, she pulled off her clothes and went to bed.

I sat in the darkness, staring out the window until Stephen lurched through the door, dead drunk. Fell into bed next to Deirdre. I heard her say: "Oh, daddy!" Then she undressed him as best she could, and they slept.

Still I sat wondering about the anguish and the anger that Shitmouth's name roused in Stephen, a sense of both love and betrayal, deepened by misunderstanding or incomprehension.

It was long past midnight when my gaze was suddenly interrupted.

Shitmouth passed the window.

Lurching.

His head, with Stephen's bandage, falling off the side of his shoulder.

His feet fumbling with the pavement.

His hands reaching for banisters in the empty air.

He seemed to stop in the midst of all his activity when he came abreast of our window.

For an instant, I felt his eyes seep into mine, hard and cold, not watery drunk. The sensation was incredible. I felt as though I were flying; that the

38

instant was an eternity, a womb for the wind. I felt full of God, and I remember thinking so clearly:

"My God! He's not lurching. He's dancing!"

And, suddenly, he was gone, leaving me with the image of a Shakespearean clown, a King's fool.

"Ask Mary."

That came back to me then.

I tiptoed out the door and up to the third floor, through dog shit, old apple cores, blackened potato peels, and the general garbage of ghetto halls. Up to the third floor to Mary's door.

I listened quietly.

There were noises inside.

Groans.

Bed creaking.

And the unmistakable snap of a whip.

I knocked.

Silence.

Then Mary's voice, the voice of dew and melon and gathering morning sun when first I had heard her, now full of piss and violent words bloated with death.

"Yeah?" What is it?"

Her voice made me shy.

"It's me. Shakey."

"Get the shit out of here! Get out of here, you hear!"

Get out of there I did.

Toward dawn, I fell asleep and dreamt a dream about the wrath of God and purifying storms.

VIII

Refreshed, I went to the crevice in the afternoon to find Shitmouth.

School was out.

The sun, heavy in the west, was spreading caramel color over the sooted banks of snow.

Approaching the crevice, I saw a group of about twenty kids, young, ten to twelve years old, hooting, jeering, jumping up and down as they rocketed snowball after snowball into the crevice.

The tranquilizers that kept them sedated in the classrooms had apparently worn off.

For an instant, I was gripped with the old fear that often overtook me when I was younger and Johnny and I had found our path blocked by such vicious mobs. But it passed quickly.

I was older now.

In control.

I crept up behind them.

Peered over their heads.

In the crevice, Mary Hynes was fucking Shit-mouth.

On top, her face buried in his neck, her bare ass, dotted with burps of snow, pounded up and down under the pelting snowballs.

They seemed oblivious to the frenzy of the mob outside the crevice. Was it then that I first caught sight of a shroud of blue over the crevice?

There was something.

A haze, possibly the sun glancing off the stone walls.

Something.

There was no time to study it.

They had begun loading the snowballs with gravel from the yard.

One of them, frothing with excitement, produced a nail, packed it into his snowball, and hollered to the rest:

"Gimme some room! I'll wing an old nail up her ass!"

Instinctively, I moved.

Collared him.

His mouth was white with foam; his eyes crazed.

I said: "Try it. I'll break your balls."

They scattered before my size. Regrouped several paces off, screaming out their disappointment, gesticulating madly at me.

I thought about running.

Turned around to find an opening.

That was all they needed to neutralize my size.

A barrage of snowballs hit me hard; the snow falling away, the gravel sticking in my skin. My head was a mass of confusion. No matter how I twined my arms around it, the stinging stones got through.

The one with the nail crept forward circling me.

Just as I stood to face him, he let fly.

I felt the nail tear into my cheek.

Tasted the blood.

Charged at him.

The pack ran out of the schoolyard as he scaled the fence and vanished. And they kept running. Home, of course, like all their little mobs, to lick their images and discover more mature forms of hatefulness and cruelty at the dinner table, where they had the benefit of counsel from their elders.

Dazed, I crumbled against the wall by the crevice.

Even now, as I finger the scar slanting above the lower jawbone on my left cheek, I remember the sensation of gagging on the blood; remember feeling the nail, large in my face, and forcing images of rust out of my mind.

My head went numb.

I knew I should try to reach Shitmouth and Mary, but I could not speak or move.

Shock had set in.

But to this day, I am certain that I did not pass

out. An ambiguity in my mind, triggered by the fact that I could not hear the sounds of their fucking. It was as though their motions were there, but they were absent.

Then there was the song that was not a song. A humming kind of lullaby coming from the crevice. A woman's voice, clean and round, rising in my ears, clouding my head with motions of red and blue, mingling, turning purple, merging into vast fields of green and surrounded by white-capped mountains. Primordial sound rolling toward the articulated form of utter beauty, toward the form of grace.

My body yearned to sleep in that sound, but it faded away, leaving only an immense block of white marble, shimmering marble, threatening to burst the horizon of my mind. I felt my hands reaching out to touch it, as though they knew how to form it, how to give body to the face of grace and deliver me into beauty forever.

But shock yanked my hands back from it.

Mary had emerged from the crevice and pulled the nail from my cheek and wadded a piece of her dress into the hole.

Yet even as I sit here today fingering the scar, I know that the song and the marble were my first real contact with the City of Light, and I am more certain than ever that it was the holy blue of the City that shrouded Shitmouth and Mary and protected them from the terror of the mob.

She said: "Come on. I'll take you to my room, and we'll work on this. Can you stand?"

"I think so."

I did.

"Put your arm around my shoulder."

I did, turning to see if Shitmouth was coming.

He was asleep, a deep smile spreading across his face.

Over his left eye, where they had been only last night, he had neither bandage nor wound.

Mary said: "Never mind."

And she lugged me down the street close on her hip, Shitmouth's odors heavy on her body.

In her cold room of broken bottles and squashed bugs, where I had fucked her one Halloween night when the police were hot on Johnny's trail, and mine, she sat me down in a rungless chair and poured a huge tumbler of whiskey. The same as she had done that night when we had come, a pace ahead of the sirens, and she had asked me what a boy brought a whore, and I had told her that I brought the memory of a girl, utterly beautiful, screaming naked in the night, which was herself, as I first saw her in the city streets.

The same as she had done long after when I brought her Shitmouth's ashes in the morning sun, and she mixed them in a tumbler of whiskey and drank them down, herself to be the urn carrying him to peace and safety and the fulfillment of his destiny.

I said: "I don't understand how you can fuck Shitmouth."

"You don,'t huh?"

"How in God's name can he get it up?"

"That's my business."

"But how can you get by the stench?"

"Stench is in the nose of the sniffer, sonny," she quipped. Then, as she wrestled my mouth open to burn the wound inside with whiskey, she added: "I come from the farms and the earth, and I have known love behind the pig sty. Shit is not far from the source of life."

After she had bandaged my cheek and satisfied herself that there was no infection, she said: "I want to thank you for helping him yesterday."

"He told you?"

"Yes. I didn't know he was hurt until this morning. Something told me his face was full of tears, and I went to him."

"What happened to his wound?"

"That is my business. It is not time for you to know, or you would already know."

And that is all she would say about it, but, in time, I would learn to see how the body, rising splendidly from the earth, heals the contingencies of the world, drives them inside, and sets the eye of man beyond reality, securing him in a deeper womb, there to shine in truth and grow in freedom.

I said: "Will you tell me about him? Stephen said I should ask you."

"Is that why you were snooping around here last night?"

"Yes."

She poured another tumbler of whiskey. Sat heavily on the edge of the naked, foul-smelling bed. The harshness seemed to melt away from her, and her eyes smiled dreamily.

"Stephen told you?"

"Yes. He said his name was Tanner, and he was pissed when I called him Shitmouth."

"He didn't tell you why?"

"No."

"Well that's Stephen," she said, smiling. "I suppose their's is a deeper relationship. Stephen knew him before all of us, except Gabriel."

45

She took a hefty belt from the tumbler and closed her eyes.

I was afraid she would get too drunk before I found out anything.

I pressed her.

"How did he know him? Where? Who is he?"

Her eyes snapped open. The harshness returned to her features. "Why do you want to know?" she asked suspiciously.

"I want to find out about him."

"Why? What fucking business is it of yours?"

"Hell, I don't know. Why is everybody protecting him? What's the big secret, anyway?" Everytime I ask a question about him, people go crazy in the face, and I learn nothing, but I know I need to find out about him. I need to talk to him. I think he knows something that Johnny knew and maybe you know and maybe Stephen. Something I think I have to know if I'm going to go any further."

She fell silent.

Outside the window, twilight walked to the edge of earth.

Finally, she said: "I keep forgetting you were Johnny's friend. But I don't know how much I should tell you. I'll tell you this: He was Stephen's professor before he dropped out."

I was stunned. "Shitmouth a professor?"

I said: "Where? At Saunsoci University?"

"Yes."

"In what?"

"Philosophy."

"What happened to him?"

"Shitmouth was booted out, and Stephen dropped out at the same time."

"Why was he booted out?"

"I don't know the details. Something about being unfit to teach. It's not important, anyway. Nothing in the past is important to anyone anymore."

"But why won't Stephen talk to me about it?"

"That's Stephen's way. Shitmouth won't talk to you about it, either. Can't you hear what I'm saying? It's just not important. There is no past for any of us anymore. The past was our murder."

She said: "You better go now. It's getting dark, and I've got business coming. We'll talk some other time."

At the door, I turned and looked at her.

She drained the tumbler.

Her shoulders sank heavily into her body, and I thought of the immensity of weariness and, again, of the incredible beauty she had been not so long ago.

She said: "Wait a minute."

Got up and fumbled at her dresser. Came to the door and took my hand. Pressed the nail into my palm.

"I don't know how much he'll tell you," she said huskily, "but you could ask Gabriel since he is still teaching up at the university."

"Gabriel? The priest?"

"Who else? How many Gabriels do you know?"

"I don't know him very well."

"Just be sure you are gentle with what you learn," she said, closing the door.

47

IX

On the way downstairs, I pondered the problem of Gabriel.

He was one of Stephen's friends; showed up periodically at the room to talk through the night about things I thought rather naive for their age, but Stephen displayed a kind of paternal benevolence toward them that he would not think of doing with Deirdre. I had presumed that they had been students together sometime in the past. Which was true, but it was some time before I learned that Gabriel had known Mary many years ago in the hills and fields around Thuddity, where they both were raised; he an orphan; she a legend.

A spare, bodiless man with limpid eyes, he was ordained a priest at twenty-two; became a professor of theology at twenty-seven. Presumed radical, he was into the Death of God movement and related things, but he struck me as a perpetual adolescent, awkward with his face and eyes, awkward with thought that moved in the higher ranges or the deeper streams. Perhaps because he did not know the body, the flesh of the body, or because he feared it, he professed the rather simple notion one day to sweep the nation in the mealy mouths of sociologists and psychologists, that evil and hatred would soon depart the earth should everyone but gaze into each other's eyes and, holding hands, whisper "thou" in each other's ears. Mindless beyond belief, naive to its very core, it was precisely the thesis the mobs needed to continue their slaughter of reflective thinkers in their midst, the slaughter that removed from all their action the requirement or the conscience of culture. Not by any accident did the individual become the arch enemy of their professions and solitude the mark of guilt. Solitude. The appearance of which, at any moment, was sufficient authority to commence a pogrom.

I had no use for Gabriel, and out of consideration for Stephen, I usually left the room or fell asleep when he showed up. The feeling was mutual. Stephen told me once that Gabriel thought I was the incarnation of evil. But at the time, and for a long time later I did not know that Gabriel had been hiding in the closet the night I fucked Mary. But all this would change between Gabriel and me. When the medallion was given to me. And later,

49

when we took Mary's broken body back to her people's earth, Stephen, Gabriel, and I.

But now, as I returned to the room, I felt that nothing could come of asking Gabriel anything, and I could not fathom the alliance that brought Stephen, Johnny, Shitmouth, Mary, and Gabriel together and excluded me.

When I entered the room, Deirdre was sitting on the bed singing to herself as she poured over a sheaf of Stephen's poems. Her hands flew to her face in shock when she saw me.

I said: "Stephen, when is Gabriel coming again?"

Bent over his typewriter, he motioned violently for me to get out.

Deirdre screamed: "Daddy! Shakey's hurt!"

He bolted from the typewriter.

Peered intently at my face.

"What the fuck happened to you?!"

I showed him the nail, the size of a spike now as I looked at it.

I said: "Snowballs."

He shook his head. Examined the bandage. Opened my mouth to satisfy himself that the bleeding had stopped.

"Who fixed this?"

"Mary."

He nodded. "I thought so. It smells like her whiskey. Looks all right to me."

I said: "I'll take off and leave you to your work."

"It doesn't matter," he muttered, waving at the typewriter. "It's ruined now, anyway."

I decided it was better to leave until his tension subsided.

"Gabriel is suppose to come tonight," Deirdre said as I backed out the door.

Shitmouth was sitting at the three-legged table by the juke box when I entered Harry's Bar and Grill. His glass was empty again. He seemed relaxed, a whisper of a smile hovering around his whiskered lips, but his hands were shaking violently, and a spasmodic shudder would intermittently sweep his whole body.

I ordered a couple of beers from Harry.

He leaned across the bar into my face. "Say," he said, "I don't want any more trouble from you two like yesterday, ya hear?"

I nodded. Paid him with money I had borrowed a week ago from Candy, who was doing well singing and panhandling on the street.

Carrying the beers back to the table, I was happy to see a flicker of recognition in Shitmouth's expression.

Sitting down, almost blushing as my eyes met his, I felt that same sensation of buoyancy, of flying, I had felt last night. Beneath the smile on his face, his eyes were cold blue, flickering white in the center with intensity and lucidity.

I pushed a beer over to him.

He tried to pick it up, but his hands shook so badly that the entire glass threatened to spill over. Beer slurped over the edge, ran down the table on to his trousers. Finally, he gave it up, bent his head down to the glass and sucked up as much as he could. When he could reach no more that way, he motioned for me to hold the glass, which I did, a little too eagerly as I recall. Finished, we went to the bar for another round.

"You expect to get a swallow, you better belt

it down fast," Harry quipped as he took my change.

Returning to the table, that is exactly what I did.

With an air of bravado, I took a big gulp and said: "Shitmouth. I want to talk to you," never thinking the name might be offensive to him because that was what Johnny and I called him in the past when we ordered him to get us a six-pack. It did not seem to bother him anymore now than it did then.

He said nothing. Just looked at me quizzically, though I could feel the hardness under his gaze in every pore of my body.

He moved a shaking finger across the table toward my face; touched the bandage.

I took the nail out of my pocket. Showed it to him.

I said: "Snowballs."

In an instant, he whisked the nail from my hand, bridged it between the index and little fingers of his right hand, bent it in half, and dropped it on the table.

My mouth fell open.

While his left hand continued shaking violently, his right hand seemed, for that instant, to arrest motion itself, not only in his hand but in me and the whole room, and as I had last night, I felt again the breath of eternity, the tug of something strange trying to carry me away; something far too demanding for my knowledge or comprehension, yet immensely intimate.

It was a moment or so, but it could have been hours, before I realized he was speaking.

He said clearly, distinctly, the pupils of his eyes flaming white: "Talk? What do you have to say?"

"I want to get drunk with you. I want to see what you see." The statement sounded ridiculous to me after I had said it, but I realized that that was exactly what I wanted to do.

Shitmouth laughed.

He said: "Whiskey."

Anxiously, I bought a bottle from Harry, who smiled and shook his head at the transaction. He said: "I don't know what yer up ta kid, but see the bottle don't leave the premises."

"The premises is what I'm up to," I quipped, returning to the table.

In the rhythm of his shakes, Shitmouth found it easier to control the bottle than the glass. He held it in the crook of his arm and lifted it to his mouth, his other hand tightly gripping the elbow.

It soon disappeared, and I returned to the bar for another.

Halfway through the second, I was shot. It was all I could do to see across the table. Shitmouth just chuckled as he watched me sink to the table.

Almost magically, an egg appeared from his pocket.

He tried to tap it, but his hands were shaking so badly that it rolled off the table on to the floor. As though in slow motion, he bent to reach it, but it again evaded him and skittered under the juke box.

On my hands and knees, I crawled after it. Around the table, through the pool of dried blood, which froze my attention for a moment, through a maze of cobwebs and dust balls under the machine, which terrorized my hand, until I felt the hardness of the egg.

How I got back to my chair, cracked, peeled, and handed him the egg, I don't know, for the strength was gone from my shoulders.

He made a cup out of his hand; tried to shovel it toward his mouth. It escaped him again. Squirted into my lap.

I fumbled with my trousers until I found it.

Shitmouth laughed gleefully.

When I got it in my hand, I tried desperately to throw it at him, but there was no strength.

Suddenly, he stopped laughing and hunched over the table, peering intently into my eyes, but my face was flowing out around the room, and his eyes seemed only pinpoints in the immensity of my swirling consciousness. But his words rose out of the swirling and quieted it so that all that was left in my head was a sensation of lightness and buoyancy.

He said: "The truth is in the egg. Who knows the sorrow of the egg? Inside the egg, I see food wrapped in loneliness."

That was all.

I held it to his blackened gums before I passed out on the table.

I did not see Gabriel enter the bar nor feel the two of them carry me home.

But somewhere in the night, I had a dream in which I was crawling toward a Gantian table piled high with food, and my body felt like a cavern of hunger, nausea, and weakness. I crawled desperately toward the table, reaching out for it, but my arms seemed to melt away just as I was about to touch it. Finally, I crawled under it and lifted it on my back. But the food, instead of falling to the floor, simply vanished, and I was overcome with fear.

I woke up slobbering.

It was the middle of the night.

I heard the murmur of voices at the foot of my mattress and gradually saw Stephen and Gabriel standing at the window talking.

They were talking about me.

Gabriel saying: "I still don't see what he's trying to prove."

"I told you. He's not trying to prove anything. He thinks he can learn something from Tanner."

"What's he going to learn dead drunk?"

I said: "Something about food, fear, and weakness."

Suddenly, I had to vomit. Bolted from the mattress. Dashed down the hall. Puked up a quart of burning yellow whiskey in pouring sweat and throbbing headache. My cheek felt like it was going to burst through the bandage and the side of my face.

"Not so smart now, are you?" Gabriel snipped when I staggered back to the mattress and collapsed, chills sweeping my body.

"Yeah, fuck you, too."

"What the hell did you think you were doing?" Stephen asked.

"See. I was trying to see."

"See what?"

"What he sees. That's all. I was just trying to see what he sees when he's stoned out of his mind."

"Tanner is never out of his mind, drunk or sober," Gabriel said.

"You damn fool!" Stephen laughed at me. "You think you can see what he sees when he's drunk. Hell, it took him years to put his eyes together inside his stupor, and you think you're going to get bombed out of the blue and reach it? You got to be kidding."

"A bit pretentious, to say the least," Gabriel sniffed.

"Yeah, well wait and see," I shouted. "What do you assholes know, anyway. I already saw something."

"What?" they chorused.

"Weakness. A strange kind of weakness that will not allow a man to touch the food he so desperately needs to live. I saw a succulent array of food and an impenetrable wall of fear and loneliness surrounding it so that it could not be touched, and the loneliness somehow made the man weaker, or is it that the weakness made the man fearful and lonely? I don't know yet . . . something I can't remember right now . . . something he said about the egg . . ."

"Hell," Stephen said, "the loneliness for food is a common alcoholic ailment. Nothing new there."

"The little match-stick girl saw the same thing," Gabriel added.

"Cute, Gabriel," I replied. "Real cute. Tell me how it escapes your notice that the little match-stick girl learned it in the ascendancy of death, learned it is a prelude to the freedom from life? How does that escape you? I want to know if it is necessary to go through utter hunger and death to find the City of Light."

"Bullshit!" Stephen thundered, causing trouble in Deirdre's dreams.

"I don't know," Gabriel said, affecting his ascetic posture. "There might be something to what he says."

"Well, if you can understand something as simple as that, you know you have to help me because Shit . . . , I mean, Tanner knows and everybody, himself included, has me blocked off. You know him, Gabriel. Mary told me you did, and you can help. And I haven't found out why you won't, Stephen, but I will. I already know you were his student."

In the dim candlelight, I could not see him blush, but I could feel the tension of it, and I was again swept by a sense of love, ambiguously mounted in betrayal.

They said nothing for a moment.

Glanced at each other.

Finally, Gabriel said: "What can I do?"

"Tell me what you know. Why did he get kicked out of the University? Why didn't he go elsewhere? What's he doing stoned all the time and living in that fucking crevice? Where did he get the quilt and the medallion? Why do I think that he is not so much killing himself as living in a strange kind of future? Everything about him looks and smells of death, yet I sense something that is making a fool of death."

"You've seen the medallion?" Stephen asked.

"Yes."

"And the quilt?" Gabriel asked.

"I saw that, too."

"That must have been a while ago," Gabriel reflected. "Some kids stole it years ago."

I said: "Johnny and I burned it one night."

"Burned it!" Gabriel exclaimed, gripping Stephen's arm. "How could the quilt be burned?"

Stephen stiffened.

He said: "Don't worry, Gabriel. It wasn't burned. The quilt is safe."

"Why should I help anyone who would even think of doing something like that?" Gabriel asked me.

"Because if it is safe, I want to see it again. Because I'm sorry about the quilt, and he won't let me touch the medallion."

"All right," Gabriel said. "I'll try to tell you what I can, but it won't be today because I've got a class in a few hours. But about the University business, there's not much I can say. It was all very secret, and I tried to get information long ago, but there were only rumors."

"Secret? Why?"

"There was some kind of big scandal in the administration, and they keep all the dossiers under lock and key, even mine. You can't get any information from them. They simply say that there were certain irregularities and that, tenured or not, it would be wise for you to drop it."

"Who has the files?"

"The Dean of Faculties."

"I'll talk to him, then."

"It won't get you anywhere. If I can't find out, how do you think you will? You're not even a member of the academic community."

"I'll find out if I have to bust their fucking files open!"

Stephen's weight shuffled uneasily in the room as the first streaks of dawn slithered across the bodies of the dead rats and woke in me the need to sleep.

"I've got to get going," Gabriel said.

Stephen said nothing.

Stood again at the window looking out on the street, his hands toying with each other behind his back.

"Gabriel," he said, "Come here a minute before you leave."

Stephen put his arm round Gabriel's shoulder, and for a moment, they silently watched the dawn grow into the gray.

"How much money in the treasury?" Stephen asked.

"About fifteen thousand," Gabriel replied.

"Well, maybe it's time."

"To open the store?"

"Yeah. The young seem to be asking the questions now. Maybe it's time."

"Whenever you want," Gabriel said. "Do you want me to ask Tanner?"

"No. Let's wait and see a while longer. The store isn't going anywhere."

Instinctively, I knew they were talking about the old bookstore across the street, which had been closed as long as I can remember but which Johnny and I use to peer into. It was always dark and empty, bursting with dust and cobwebs except for the cash register, which was always shined. Johnny told me he had once seen his father in there talking to the beautiful and, to me, forever enigmatic woman of the City.

The place, I was to learn before long, where Shitmouth got his quilt of many colors.

And in time, did the young not create ten thousand such places across the land to bring the glory of the light to the moment of craft? Did they release in the knuckled fist of commerce the soft hand, tooling old but unfamiliar things?

They did.

And were there some who did not keep the faith? Who forsook the light to stand in the darkness of the old ways?

Far too many.

Far too many.

X

At dusk, I woke.

Stephen and Deirdre were gone.

Outside the window, minorities began to shift and move, casting fierce glances into the remaining light as they waited for the dark to claim their center and dissolve reality in paroxysm.

Sleep had drained away my hangover, and I was ready for another encounter with Shitmouth.

Broke, I searched the streets for Candy.

A black beret stopped me.

He said: "Hey, man, I seen you around here."

"Yeah, I'm a couple blocks over."

"Bad night for whitey. Better get off the streets."

"Why?"

"A word to the wise," he drawled, shuffling on.

I cut across town into the factory section, the aromas of roasting coffee and baking bread tantalizing the stars, upwind from the stench of the meat-packing plants. South over the railroad tracks, I turned down to the river, then north to the cove, where Johnny, Tarinia, and I had come so often when we were younger.

North to the cove, where I had learned so much about the sun and where I had seen the bird of fire plummet from the sky, beheaded by Johnny's gun.

Candy knew of the place. We had brought her here a number of times to sit and listen to her form her songs.

She was there now.

Sitting by a tree, her guitar in her lap.

Her head was curled into her shoulder. She seemed to be sleeping.

The cove was so quiet you could hear the thawed snow crystalizing with the cold of the night.

But the river was infected with the cancer of man. It smelled like Shitmouth.

And Candy wasn't sleeping.

She was quietly crying.

As I drew near, I could see the tears glistening, icing on her cheeks; her long blonde hair frazzled around her shoulders and down her back, whisps caught in the bark of the tree.

I said: "Candy?"

She did not reply.

I sat down beside her. Disentangled her hair from the bark; folded her in my arms.

Against my thin chest, her face broke down, shook with virgin sobbing; tears not yet aged in the body, not yet the hellish scream of the woman grown and enslaved by the finitude of men.

In a little while, I said: "Tell me about it."

"Oh, Shakey, what is going to happen to us?" She said: "There is no beauty in my life."

"I don't know, Candy. There is no beauty in my life, either. I guess the whole world has just run out of beauty, or maybe it never had it at all. Maybe terror is all there has ever been."

She said: "Everything around me is broken and dirty and mean. I feel so terribly empty, I just don't know what to do but die."

"What about your songs? They're beautiful, aren't they?"

"People say they are, but I think they're as empty as I am. They are not me, not the real me."

"What is that, Candy?"

"I don't know. I want to be beautiful inside, not empty like this."

"Well, why don't you get fucked and listen to the orgasm?"

She broke out of my arms.

Leaned back against the tree.

"You talk like all the rest," she snapped.

"Maybe I do, but just remember, the emptiness is inside you. It's in your body. What will fill the emptiness must also be in your body. You can't separate the two without going crazy."

"Is that the way you fill the emptiness?"

"Mine is different from yours. My emptiness

is in front of my face, not inside me. When I write, when I am deep in the garden of my plays, with the sun and the wind, and I can get man and all of his crap out from in front of my face, the emptiness disappears, and everything is safe and peaceful again, but it is not yet beauty."

"I just don't understand."

"Neither do I. But I will, Candy, I will. In the meantime, I'm broke. Loan me some money."

She fumbled in her coat.

Gave me a ten.

I said: "See you later."

"Yeah."

At the railroad tracks, I turned and went back. She had begun strumming softly.

I said: "You know I just remembered something. I was taking a shit the other day, and someone had scrawled a line from Genet on the wall: "Ugliness is only beauty at rest." Maybe it's not a question of filling the emptiness but only of waking the beauty."

"How, Shakey?"

"Damn if I know. Ugliness might simply be closed eyes. How would you waken closed eyes?"

"Sing to them."

"No. You sing to close them."

"Kiss them?"

"Sleeping Beauty? I never thought of that. I don't remember the details of the story well enough to see what happened there. Do you?"

"No."

"I know this: A nightmare that drives rest to the point of death will open closed eyes."

"My life is already a nightmare."

"I know. So is mine. So was Johnny's, but he

woke beauty. Maybe Shitmouth, too. It's getting late. I got to go find him."

Running back to the ghetto, I was possessed of a sense of weakness about that conversation with Candy. In one frozen moment, I found it. Beauty belongs to evening and always has. It is joy that belongs to waking and the morning of the eye, not beauty.

But there was no time to pursue it.

The city exploded in sirens of every description, and the skyline glowed with muted flames and smoke.

Two blocks from Harry's, I could see that the trouble was deeper down in the ghetto, a good four blocks away, but the sounds of shooting and popping glass were loud in my ears. Purple shadows darted around me in and out of alleys with armfuls of loot. Tear gas seeped like pestilence down the street. It was a simple thing. The minorities had opened a hole in the silence of darkness and poured into it the scream of life.

I pulled my coat over my head and ran for the bar. Shitmouth was at his usual place.

"How far away are they?" Harry asked.

"Four blocks and moving fast."

"Hell," he said. "They'll never get this far tonight. Whatta ya want?"

"A bottle."

"Didn't have enough of that last night, huh? Well, it's your funeral."

On the way back to the table, I decided to pace myself and not get as drunk as I had last night.

For some strange reason, Shitmouth was not shaking. His body was quiet, but his face was pursed.

He reached across the table and took the bottle from me. Uncapped it and took a gulp. Then he set the bottle in the center of the table and leaned back in his chair, motioning for me to drink.

I took a sip.

He said: "I see you have tenacity. Is it the tenacity of a fool?"

"No. But it might be the freedom of a fool."

"How do you know that?"

"I've seen you dance in the night."

He smiled.

Gulped again from the bottle.

Set it down forcefully.

He said: "Did you hold the egg to the light?"

I said: "I had a dream about the loneliness of food that left me full of fear."

"Tell me."

I recounted the dream I had last night.

He said: "You did not listen very well." And, again, from somewhere in his rags, an egg popped into his hands.

"Your dream," he said, "was a dream of the loneliness for food that fills your belly on the flat face of the world. What I said to you was that the loneliness is inside the egg with the truth. If there is an egg in your dream, it is scrambled up in a jumble of other things."

He reached across the table.

Put the egg in my hand.

Took another shot from the bottle and leaned back in his chair.

I felt like the table was completely isolated in the world, surrounded and set apart by a wall of sobriety.

He said: "Study the egg and tell me what you

see in it because the day may come when you enter it, and another may come when you will scream to leave it, and maybe it will all happen on the same day, possibly even the same instant."

I looked at the egg.

Turned it over and over.

I could see nothing but an egg.

My eyes felt dull and heavy because of the lightness that seemed to encircle the table.

I said: "I don't see anything but an egg. Can you show me how to get into it?"

"Yes, but it won't mean anything to you until you have done it by yourself."

"Show me."

He said: "I have heard that there is an old Indian, a Yaqui holy man who talks about the crack between the worlds."

Shitmouth was talking about Don Juan, whose teachings were eventually brought from the desert to the streets by Castaneda and who taught that to be a man of knowledge, one must go into the crack between the worlds, but that if one went too far into that crack without the proper help, he would be lost forever.

I said: "I know the crack. I've seen it, but I've not been in it all the way."

Shitmouth peered intently at the egg.

"There is another crack," he said softly, almost a whisper.

I leaned across the table to catch his words, my ear close to his mouth.

He said: "Far up in the crack between the worlds, at the point where it opens on the vast, there is a right turn, and suddenly you are in the crack behind the worlds."

My head was full of darkness as his finger trailed smoothly over the shell, mapping out the crack behind the worlds.

"And down that crack," he continued, there is another right turn, instantaneous, imperceptible, but when you have touched that turn, your eye will open inside the cosmic egg."

Pulling my ear from his mouth, my eyes traveled to his face to fathom his meaning.

Large tears were rolling down his cheeks on to his hands, the egg, and the table.

Overwhelmed by waves of my stupidity, I could not see what he was seeing that was so full of grief.

Grabbing the bottle, I chug-lugged it, searing my throat.

"Once inside the egg," Shitmouth said, "all the cracks and turns evaporate. There is no way out, no matter how hard you lunge at the inside of the shell. From that moment on, you are damned to see the world from the inside out, an incredible tapestry of translucent color and movement always seen from behind."

"But where is the sorrow in that?" I asked, thinking vaguely of the joy the ancients seemed to have experienced with the egg.

"The sorrow is simple. It is in the sameness of everything; a sameness that has never been ruptured in the growth of man."

I said: "Shitmouth, the ancients talked about the cosmic egg, but they felt it could be broken, and they found joy in that."

"The ancients were never inside the egg," he replied. "They saw the egg always from the outside, and their task was to justify and glorify what is. The egg is easily broken when it is seen from the outside."

His hand smashed down on the egg.

It was not hard-boiled.

The yolk spread out over the table.

He said: "To break the egg from the outside is to destroy the meaning of the inside. It is suicide or murder. It is always destructive and will saturate everything with destruction."

"But isn't it madness to stay on the inside and not get out?"

"It is complete insanity if you do not know how to sit quietly and wait for sorrow to grow into beauty. The task is no longer to justify what is but to justify what is not yet, for the meaning of the inside of the egg is the quest for life growing and growing until it shatters the shell from the need for its life to be made manifest and, perhaps, beget more life."

He said: "The City of Light is inside the egg."

He said: "God is inside the egg delivering beauty out of sorrow through his quiet building."

Shitmouth produced another egg from his pocket, cupped it in his hands.

He seemed very young.

Childlike.

And his throat was full of laughter.

He said: "There will be heat from the outside to help the inside grow."

"What is so great that its brooding can hatch the cosmic egg?" I asked.

"The heat that is generated from the decomposition of everything that is," he replied. "The cauldron of terror that has become the heat and the heart of reality."

Suddenly, his face froze.

He jerked.

"What's this?" he whispered.

Bent his ear to the egg.

"My God!" he exclaimed. "Someone is screaming in the City of Light."

I started to ask what he meant, but he motioned violently for me to be quiet and pressed the egg closer to his ear.

He said: "It is your friend Johnny and his father."

A wave of terror swept his face as I reached for the egg.

I pressed it close to my ear.

I heard nothing but my own pulse.

The door of the bar crashed open.

A dozen black, brown, and red berets stormed through, heavily armed.

One shouted to Harry: "Lock it up! The pigs are comin'."

Harry ran to the door, bolted it, and pulled the shade.

A beret turned to us: "Git the fuck outta here, whitey!"

I said: "Fuck off, we're talking."

A rifle bolt slammed home in front of my face.

"Git upstairs. I'll take care of 'em!" Harry shouted.

They filed behind the bar, into the kitchen. I heard the thud of boots mounting stairs.

Harry dashed to the table.

Grabbed both of us by the back of the neck. Propelled us to the door. Opened it and pitched us headlong into the street.

Mobs were running everywhere.

They caught Shitmouth up in a stampede while I crouched against the wall. He was still holding the egg to his ear.

Coldly silent and doubled over as if I had been shot, I sidled down the block to the tenement. Bolted through the door of the room and pulled the shade. Deirdre was sound asleep. Stephen was gone.

My stomach in knots, exhausted from tension but fearful of losing what I had heard, I sat in a corner of my mattress and forced myself to remember everything he had said.

Gradually, I dozed into a half sleep, half dream in which I sat in a spacious marble room listening to the pulse of the sea and a child speaking wide words.

Stephen shattered the dream.

He burst through the door, shouting: "Shakey! Shakey! Gimme a hand!"

He was carrying a puppet in his arms, a guitar strung over his back.

It was Candy.

Naked and a mass of blood.

Raped.

Dierdre screamed.

Crawled into the corner of her mattress.

Cowered with her hands over her face.

Candy's head was twisted under Stephen's arm as though her neck was broken.

Stephen laid her on the mattress, his face gurgling tears.

Fumbled for his medical kit, his hands blinded with terror and anguish.

Did the world stop in the flow of giant Stephen's tears?

It was never seen before.

Has not been seen since.

Yes, I think the world stopped.

But all I remember is standing there looking down at her, unable to recognize or feel anything but the sweat pouring down me, cold, my head and body totally frozen.

Condensing.

Dead.

Suddenly, Stephen screamed: "Get Mary!"

Then he kicked me. Hard. And pain shot through me, opening a fissure in the ice.

I fled to the door, which seemed a world away.

Mary was already there.

Quietly, she pushed Stephen aside. Bent over Candy. Straigtened her head and examined the cuts and bruises and the patch of flesh on her head, where a mass of hair had been torn out.

Then she reached across the bed and slapped Deirdre hard in the face.

She said: "Deirdre! Get some cloth! You," she said to me, "get down the hall and get some warm water."

Deirdre moved out of the corner.

I shot down the hall with a pan and ran the hot water until it burned my hand. Filled the pan. Ran back.

Mary said: "Stephen! Get your face together. I'm gonna need help here."

He did.

Shook his head violently.

Said: "God Almighty!"

Commenced rummaging in his kit for ointments and bandages while Mary gently dabbed the wounds.

She said: "All right, now, tell me what happened."

Stephen's voice cracked: "I was down by the river, and I heard her singing far away, and then I heard her screaming. By the time I got there, they were running off. Eight or ten of them, I couldn't tell."

Mary moved down the mattress. Opened Candy's legs. Great globs of sperm and blood oozed out.

She said: "Mary Mother of God!"

Then she turned to me: "Upstairs and get my douche bag and fill it with warm, not hot, water."

"Douche bag?"

"It's hanging on the bedpost. Get!"

And so they labored over her, Stephen and Mary, for what seemed like hours while I stood helplessly by and began to fill with screams, my hands aching for Johnny's gun.

He entered so quietly, it was a few minutes before I realized he was there.

Shitmouth.

He leaned over Stephen and Mary and studied Candy's body.

Then, almost imperceptibly, he put his hands on their shoulders, and they melted away from her so that he stood there alone.

Clearly, unmistakably, in Big Sam's voice, he said: "This is my daughter."

The room was a tomb of quiet.

Clearly, unmistakably, in Johnny's voice, he said: "This is my sister."

Then he knelt by the mattress, and pulling an

73

egg from his rags, he touched her lips with it.

Finally, he turned to Stephen and Mary. He said: "Let the child hold the egg."

They nodded.

Gathered around him.

Shitmouth handed the egg to Deirdre.

Brought the medallion out of his rags.

Mary produced a candle from between her breasts.

Lit it.

Held it between Candy's legs.

She said: "The insult in your womb will become the fountain of your dreams."

And again there was the unusual flame, like the candle she lit the night Johnny was electrocuted.

A haze of blue covered Shitmouth and Mary, Deirdre and Candy.

But not Stephen.

Nor I.

On every cut and bruise and burn, Shitmouth laid the medallion, and one by one they vanished.

He turned to Stephen. "She will need the quilt for a while."

Stephen said: "I'll get it."

Left the room.

I thought I was losing my mind.

At the window, I saw him cross the street and enter the bookstore, but to this day, I do not remember seeing him open the door.

When he returned, he had the quilt of many colors that Johnny and I had burned years ago.

I burst with joy.

Shitmouth rose.

He said: "Where will she sleep?"

Stephen motioned toward my mattress.

"Place her there."

He did.

Awe-struck, I watched Shitmouth cover her completely with the quilt; take the candle from Mary and stand it by the mattress. The quilt glowed like a fresh rainbow in the room, the rainbow of the Covenant.

At the door, Deirdre ran to Shitmouth. Kissed him. Handed him back the egg.

Stephen shifted uneasily.

As he turned to leave with Mary, Shitmouth stared at me for a moment.

He said: "Of course, if you talk about what you have seen and heard tonight, they will only laugh."

Then they were gone.

And Stephen, Deirdre, and I fell asleep together.

I do not think that in all my life I ever slept so deeply.

There were no dreams.

XI

Smiling:
Dizzy with the excitement of new things, I searched the rubble of the streets for Shitmouth for over a week while the candle burned and the hue of the rainbow grew deeper in the room. He was nowhere to be found. Nor Mary.

Neither Stephen nor I could get by the rainbow to check on Candy, but Deirdre walked through it without hesitation and reported on the patterns of her breathing until we were satisfied that she was living and healing.

Haunted by their absence in the street, my smile drew into a frown, and I noticed that the rainbow was losing its brilliance and assuming the vile colors of the room.

On the tenth day, the candle evaporated, and the rainbow vanished.

And winter warmed into spring, and the calls of the first birds.

I went to the crevice.

Sat and waited.

The hours passed into days.

Still he did not come, and hunger forced me to abandon my vigil.

When I returned to the room, Candy was sitting in the middle of my mattress strumming her guitar.

The quilt was gone.

Stephen was back working at his typewriter.

Candy smiled when I entered.

Her face flushed.

Radiant.

I kissed her.

She said: "Hi, Shakey."

"Hi, beautiful."

Stephen halted at the typewriter.

He said: "Candy will be staying with us now."

I said: "Good." Ladled out a bowl of stew. Ate.

I said: "Stephen, what happened to the quilt?"

"It's safe. Where have you been the last couple of days?"

"At the crevice waiting for Shitmouth and Mary. They've disappeared."

Candy said: "They are in the City of Light."

"You were there?"

"For a long time. I saw Daddy and Mom and Johnny and Tarinia."

She said: "There are so many people there. Johnny said to tell you to come and visit for a while, and Mommy said to say hello."

At the window, I stared at the shattered street. Trying to think how under the quilt she had gotten there as on a magic carpet. Nothing would focus except my own sense of being left out.

She said: "Shitmouth showed me all over the City."

"We don't use that name here," Stephen snapped.

"Shut the fuck up, Stephen!" I yelled.

She said: "Everywhere we went, people came up to us and gave him things they had made. They called him Sayer. Everything was so quiet and beautiful, like a dream under water, and he took everything they gave him up to the mountain and put it all into the fire of the Law."

"Why would he do that?"

"The people wanted him to speak."

"Did they follow him to the mountain?"

"No. After they gave him the things they had made, they all went back into their own homes, and when everything was gone in the fire, he stood up behind the light, and he talked. You could hear his voice all over the City."

"Where was Mary?"

"I only saw her once. She went into the temple in the center of the City, and I didn't see her again. Here. I'll show you."

Candy held out her guitar.

She said: "Look between the strings."

Stephen moved from his typewriter.

Leaned over my shoulder.

There in the drum of the guitar was a shimmering replica of the City. The same that was on Shitmouth's medallion.

She said: "There in the center, is the building Mary went in."

A cone-shaped building, wide at the bottom, narrow at the top; the tip open to the sky and beyond.

As I looked at it closely, it seemed like all the houses in the City formed the base of the cone.

Stephen trembled.

Took the guitar from my hands. Peered into it intently, his eyes glistening.

He said: "Where did you get this?"

"It was here when I woke up."

"Did you have your guitar in the City?"

Yes.

"Did you play it?"

"For Johnny and Tarinia. Then Shitmouth took it away from me and threw it in the fire with everything else."

Once again, I had the eerie sensation that something had snapped in my head and my mind was seeping into darkness.

I said: "What did he say when he spoke behind the fire?"

"I only remember a little. He talked for a long time. He said everything was good and that there was great beauty in everything he had been given but that it was only a beginning and that if people truly listened to the Law inside themselves, there would be even greater beauty. He talked about the body as the center of all creation and how each person must love themselves so deeply that out of their solitude beauty would come like a natural flower and be an eternal gift to the City and the truth of the Law. He talked about a lot of other things I could not understand."

"What did the people say?"

"Nothing."

"Nothing at all?"

She said: "There was a song that seemed to rise out of every house, but not really a song, more like a chant, a sound like I've never heard. It made my insides melt, and I felt like I was floating in it. Then I woke up."

"Can you sing it?"

"No."

But she would one day, and the tribes would gather from across the nation to hear her singing naked before the moon and themselves come to the certainty of things.

"Was he wearing his rags in the City?" I asked.

"No. He wasn't wearing anything."

"He was naked?"

She said: "I don't know. I just don't remember him wearing anything."

Suddenly, a movement across the street caught my eye outside the window.

Shitmouth and Mary were walking away from the front of the bookstore.

I could not fathom what sense of reality caused me to murmur: "They're back."

By the time I got to the bar, he was already sitting at his table.

He looked old.

Exhausted.

I sat down, my mind drowning in my face.

"I was waiting for you," I blurted.

"I was busy."

"Candy said you were teaching in the City of Light."

Shitmouth waved the statement aside wearily.

He said: "How is she?"

"Smiling."

His eyes closed; his face relaxed.

How much time passed, I can't remember. It did not seem important. I felt myself falling asleep in the chair until my eyes inside my head formed around the gleaming image of the City in the drum of the guitar, and I could feel tears birthing on my face miles away.

It was desperation.

The need to go, to be there:

To sit in the wide winds and be clean and strong and full of listening.

But my shoulders were weak; made even more so by the colossal strength I could feel pouring from Shitmouth.

I think it was in that moment that I first began to see and feel what he was doing with the booze. It was a simple thing. When he returned from the City, all his power dissipated in reality, and to stop the flow of that energy at the moment where it would extinguish all he meant to life, he sealed reality off in darkness and nothingness, damned it to its course, and, in so doing, kept the light alive inside himself and went on building, shrouded from the gaze of the dreamless by a thick, quilted haze.

Shaking.

My body a web of trembles, I reached across the table and shook him gently.

"Eh? What is it?"

His eyes opened slowly.

White heat poured out into the room.

Dissolved the table.

Nothing was between us.

Leaning over, I took his hand.

"Shitmouth," I whispered hoarsely, "will you take me to the City of Light."

"No."

"But why not? You took Candy?"

He said: "She went by herself. I only met her there."

"But you left at the same time."

"Yes, but by a different way. Everybody has their own way. When they find it, they'll get there. You can not take someone else's way without getting lost. Only your own."

"Your way is at the beginning of your energy and therefore of your love. Find that and you will find the path."

"Shitmouth," I said helplessly, "I have never loved anything. All my life is hate."

He said: "You have loved. Hate is not possible unless there has first been great love and great betrayal. You must go into the very center of hate and find the betrayal that soured your love."

I had the awesome feeling that he was telling me to go crazy.

Without my seeing how it happened, the medallion was in my hand.

He said: "What do you see?"

"An image of the City."

"Look closer."

There seemed to be movement at the top of the cone as though something was trying to break out.

He said: "Look slowly!"

A huge bird struggled out of the cone. Perched on the edge. It was a golden hawk. It spread its wings. Flew straight toward me.

I had the unmistakable sensation that the earth had just split asunder.

I vaguely remember screaming.

Turned away.

Shitmouth took the medallion from me.

He said: "Well?"

"I saw a huge bird, a hawk flying straight at my face."

He said: "The hawk will lead you to the beginning of your path. Follow the hawk.

"What the fuck's goin' on here," Harry shouted in my ear. "What's all the screamin' about back here?"

My tongue stumbled in my mouth.

The light vanished.

The table swam back into focus.

"Nothing," I mumbled. "It's nothing, Harry."

"Yeah, well you assholes goin' get the D.T.'s, get 'em somewhere else ya hear."

"Yeah, yeah sure."

Shitmouth closed his eyes.

Slept.

My eyes wide open, my mind dissolved in the spray of dried blood on the floor.

Then darkness came.

The noises in the bar, the greasy light and smoke, cut through the wall of my solitude.

Out in the street, the breeze was warm.

Gentle.

Like the flutter of wings.

XII

The next morning, I decided it was time to check out the university.

A huge complex of concrete on a hill overlooking Saunsoci.

Twenty-five to thirty thousand students.

Once there, it took me about an hour to find Gabriel's office in the Department of Theology.

He was bent over a bound manuscript.

Motioned me toward a chair.

Continued reading.

He looked smaller, more frail behind the desk than he did in our room. The manuscript seemed to engulf him.

Carpeted in pale blue, the walls lined with rickety metal bookcases filled with hundreds of books sporting pious, innocuous titles, the office smelled of air-conditioned dust. It surpassed the imagination to conceive of any profound thought ever being born in the place.

In time, he chuckled and closed the manuscript.

"By heavens!" he exclaimed. "Here's a fellow trying to get a dissertation through by proving that Judas was a genius and loved Christ. He claims that, historically, Judas became the least of them and is, therefore, first in the Kingdom of Heaven."

Pushing the manuscript aside, he said: "It'll be rejected, of course. No precedent for that sort of thinking."

I said: "I came to see the Dean about Shitmouth."

His eyes narrowed.

He said: "I thought you had given up that foolishness."

"I saw the quilt again."

Gabriel was silent.

Stared at me.

"Yes," he said weakly, "I know. I dropped by to see Candy. How is she?"

"She went to the City and came back. Shitmouth and Mary went with her."

Gabriel did not respond.

His limpid, watery eyes shifted past my face.

Fixed on the window.

I said: "You told me you would help."

"I told you there was nothing I could do. I can't get any information from them."

"Then take me to him."

"I'll show you where his office is, but I'm not going to get involved. There's too much at stake."

At the time, I did not know what he meant and cursed his weakness. Later, I was to learn that a considerable part of his salary was being set aside in trust to finance the opening of the bookstore across the street from us in order that creations from the City of Light might find their way into the streets.

I said: "Let's go."

We walked across the campus to a ten-story glass-walled building filled with hundreds of administrators and clerks. Guards were posted at the entrance, but they did not try to stop us from entering. The days of their duty had not yet come.

But it would.

When we reached the third floor, Gabriel stopped.

He said: "This is as far as I go. His office is at the end of the hall."

"What's his name?"

"Dean Flagrant," he flung over his shoulder as he squirted down the staircase.

Cutting through the din of typewriters and computers, I approached his door at the end of the hall.

Gold stenciling: Dr. B. S. Flagrant, Dean of Faculties.

I knocked.

A door closed inside.

"Come in! Come in!" The voice, distant and harsh.

I opened the door.

Entered.

It was an incredibly spacious room, walnut paneling, deep-piled orange carpeting. A walnut conference table with nickel-plated legs and a dozen black-leather swivel chairs arrayed around sat to the right. File cabinets banked the left wall and far down in the center, against the windows, a huge walnut desk and a tall man with steel-gray hair standing behind it in a gray pin-stripe suit.

It was a room of importance.

Intimidating.

I felt strength ebbing from my legs and sensed that my face was losing firmness of purpose.

"Yes, yes." he motioned. "Come right on in. You know my door is always open to students."

He was all smiles as I made my way into the depth of the room and sat down in front of the desk.

As he sat down, I noticed that he opened the right-hand drawer of the desk and pushed a button.

It was a tape recorder.

Reaching across the desk to shake my hand, he said: "You must be new. I don't think we've met before. I'm Dean Flagrant."

"Shakey," I mumbled.

A brief, quizzical flash in his eyes. His nose sniffing the air.

"Well," he said. "No matter. What have you come to report, and I do wish you people would take a bath before you come in here."

At that, he produced an aerosol can and commenced spraying air freshener around.

I had become so use to the odors of our room, it never occurred to me that my clothes were saturated with the smell of the dead rats and rotting fruit.

The can disappeared into the desk.

"Now that's better," he smirked. "Well, out with it. What is your report?"

I said: "I'm not a student."

"Not a student, not a student," he repeated. "Well, then, what in heaven's name are you here for?"

His hand hovered over the tape recorder as though he were going to shut it off. Thought better of it. Leaned back in his chair, folding his hands over his belly.

I said: "I've come to see you about a friend of mine who taught here. I want some information about him."

"What kind of information?"

"Why he was fired, for one thing."

His hands unfolded. His chair snapped back to attention at his desk.

"Fired! Fired! Who is this friend of yours?"

"Shit . . . I mean, Tanner. Robert Tanner."

His face darkened His right hand stroked his chin as he searched his memory for the name.

I said: "He taught Philosophy a few years ago."

The Dean's face reddened. His hand twitched on his chin.

"Yes," he said. "I remember the case. One of the worst we've had to deal with. You don't have very nice friends."

"Why was he fired?"

Administrative paranoia seeped forward in his face. His shoulders stiffened. His voice became haughty, arrogant.

"There were irregularities. Yes, indeed, a considerable number of irregularities."

"Like what?"

"I'm afraid we don't discuss these matters."

"You won't tell me."

"Of course not!" he exclaimed indignantly.

"Then at least let me look at your files so I can see for myself."

"Look at my files?" He laughed. "Well, I must say, young man, you're either extremely naive or crazy. Our files are secret. Only the President and myself examine them. Look at my files?! Indeed! You just get on out of here now."

I stood up.

Schooled in America, I shouted American truth:

"Hell! This is a public institution supported by public taxes, and your files are open to examination the same as every other public institution."

He stood up.

Came to power in America himself.

Shouted the truth of that power.

"I am the Dean!"

Dead silence for a moment as we confronted each other.

He pulled a red phone out of the desk.

"Now you get out of here this moment, or I'll call the guards."

I marched out of the depth of the room.

At the door, I turned.

"Dean!" I shouted. "Hell, you're nothing but a fucking spook!"

He lifted the receiver as I slammed the door.

Out on the mall, I sat in the spring grass and the sun and pondered the problem.

There was no other solution.

I would have to break into the files.

But how, without being seen?"

I walked back to Gabriel's office.

He was gone.

On the way back to the Administration building to case the third floor, I saw a fight in the center of the mall.

A half-dozen blacks were pummeling a white student, whose books and papers were scattered all around on the grass.

As I drew near, I could hear them shouting: "Ya burned us, mother fuckin' honky! Ya burned us."

Hundred of students wandered by without so much as glancing at them.

When he fell to the ground, a mass of pulp and protruding bones, they ripped off his clothes and went through the pockets.

"I got it, man, I got it!" one of them shouted, holding up a bundle of white packets.

Then they ran.

I walked over to him.

Looked down.

His face beyond repair, his balls had been kicked back up into his body.

Putting steel in my face, I walked on by.

Back on the third floor, I found a men's room near the Dean's office that became my headquarters for a week and from which I was able to observe the patterns of his comings and goings.

The Dean was a paragon of consistency.

Every morning, he unlocked the door at precisely 8:30.

Locked it every afternoon at 4:30.

On the third, fourth, and fifth day of my surveillance, I grew bolder. Pressed my ear to his door at 4:20 every afternoon.

For three days, at precisely 4:25, I heard a door slam inside his office.

I concluded he had his own toilet. Drained himself before he locked up. I also concluded that, that would be his undoing.

But I did not yet know how.

On the fifth day, I drew a diagram of the lower half of the hall and went back to my room.

Candy and Deirdre were singing together.

Naked on my mattress.

Deirdre becoming a girl; Candy with the completeness of woman rising heavily in her body.

Stephen was not there.

I sat down at the typewriter.

Perched my diagram on the roller and studied it.

The obvious ploy was there all along.

A woman's room directly across from the Dean's office.

At 4:29 on any given day, all I needed was a decoy.

My attention was drawn to the song that Deirdre and Candy were practicing. I hadn't heard it before. It sounded like a circle undulating far away, making color in the lost caverns of the wind.

When they paused, I said: "What's that?"

"Daddy's new poem," Deirdre beamed. "Do you like it?"

"Yeah. It's beautiful."

They smiled.

I said: "Candy, come here a minute and look at this."

I felt her pubic hair whispering on my arm.

Instant hard-on.

But I could never fuck Candy. Johnny stood between us with huge fists clenched in my face.

She said: "What is it?"

I pointed to the Dean's office.

"That's where the files are that I have to get into. And over here is the men's room, and here, right here in front of his door, is the women's room."

"So?"

"I want you to help me."

"How?"

"Monday afternoon at exactly 4:29, when he comes out of his office, I want you to walk naked out of the women's room and run to the men's room. I'll be hiding in the women's room and as soon as he moves after you, I'll split into his office. We'll stash some clothes for you in the men's room."

"What if somebody's in there?"

"There won't be. Hasn't been anybody in there all week between four and four-thirty."

"What if he follows me in?"

"He won't. He's a damn spook. Even if he does, he'll hesitate at the door long enough for you to get dressed. What he'll probably do is go back to his office and call the guards. That's when you take off. By then, I'll be in the can in his office."

"I could still get caught."

"If you do, which I think is a pretty far-out possibility, just start screaming rape. He'll have you dressed and out of there in a minute. Will you do it?"

"It's pretty important, huh?"

"Yeah."

"OK. I'll try."

Stephen objected.

Deirdre told him of our plans when he returned with his arms full of fruit and vegetables.

The week's supply.

As he munched his stew, he frowned.

Ominously silent.

When his bowl clattered to the floor, the pronouncement came.

He said: "Shakey, if you do this thing, you're going to have to move out of here."

"What the hell for?"

"You'll bring the cops down around our ears, and they'll hustle Deirdre off to one of their rat traps just like they did with her mother. They're only waiting for an excuse, and I'm damned if you're going to get us involved in your bullshit."

I did not feel the terror of loss I had felt when he suggested that I leave before.

Winter was over.

Summer near.

And the need for air and bedding down by the swift streams.

I said: "So be it."

"You're still going through with it?"

"Do you have to ask?"

"What about Candy?"

"What about her?"

"She'll have to leave, too, if you get her involved."

Candy smiled at me.

We had been together too long for anything
to disturb the flow of our understanding.

She said: "I go with Shakey."

I said: "Stephen, don't you think it's about
time you told me the real reason."

"What do you mean?"

"You're not worried about cops or Deirdre.
You've been hiding something from me all along.
You're afraid I'm going to find out something
about you, aren't you?"

"You're crazy."

And that was that.

Stephen twitched and rolled into the corner
of his mattress with Deirdre.

Slept.

As did I.

But not Candy.

Her thrashing about woke me long after the
moon had made its ascent and bathed the room in
blue light.

She was masturbating.

Groaning.

Thumping.

Splaying out.

I said: "Jesus Christ, Candy! How do you
expect me to sleep with you jerking off all night?"

Across the room, Stephen sat up.

He whispered: "Candy, come here."

In a few minutes, Deirdre was sleeping by
my side.

Another few, and sounds of immense passion
spurted into the blue light of the moon.

Followed by a long sigh.

Silence.

And then song.

It was the same song I had heard at the crevice the day Mary fucked Shitmouth.

Again, a block of shimmering white marble rose in my head, and I saw the earth rising from its center to the likeness of the moon.

Deirdre snuggled into my arms.

"Do you hear the music?" she whispered. "Isn't it beautiful?"

"Yes. It's beautiful.

But I also thought that Stephen was trying to wrest Candy away from me.

XIII

Whatever, it didn't work.

Four twenty-five Monday:

Candy and I were at our stations in the women's room across from the Dean's office.

I said: "Make sure he doesn't get a chance to turn the key. Don't even give him a chance to put it in the lock."

"OK."

Four twenty-eight, the Dean stepped into the hall, and I whacked Candy on the butt.

Out she went.

Got his face bewildered.

His hand froze in an arc at the lock.

Then she ran down the hall.

For a moment, it seemed as though he wouldn't take the bait, and I thought that I should have had her walk instead of run.

As it was, it turned out for the best.

By the time he finished blustering around with his comprehension and followed after her, Candy was already in the men's room, and he didn't see her enter.

And I was securely hidden behind the door of his john.

He returned, as I thought he would, and called the guards. "My God!" he bellowed into the phone. "There's a naked woman running around up here on three. I want her found immediately!"

Candy, I figured, would probably be going out the front door as they were hanging up the phone.

It was five o'clock before I finally heard him lock the door, and I crept out into his office. I remember having the strange feeling that I was some kind of mad scientist in the medieval world, stealthily digging up cadavers under the cover of darkness to learn the most elementary facts about the human anatomy, which were on the Index then to be sure, as the human soul is now.

The files were locked, of course, and it was another hour before I found the master key under the tape recorder in his drawer and unlocked the T files.

Under Tanner, there was a huge manila envelope and a box of tapes.

Returning with them to the desk, I thumped with excitement.

Opened the envelope and spread the papers out.

The first one was dated ten years ago and was headed:

"Final Disposition: Case of Robert T. Tanner, Assistant Professor, Department of Philosophy."

The heading was followed by a single terse statement:

"Purchased the remaining two years of a five-year contract for the sum of thirty thousand dollars."

There followed three contracts signed by Shitmouth and the President of the University. The first was for three years, dated seventeen years ago and specifying that he was to teach three courses in Introductory Philosophy for $8,500. The second contract represented an extension of the first, dating from his second year. It was to run for three years and specified that he was to teach one undergraduate course in the History of Philosophy and two graduate seminars: Problems in Aesthetics and Problems in Ontology for $10,500. The third specified the same as the second except the salary had jumped to $15,000.

Shitmouth had apparently found favor in the eyes of Academie somewhere along the way. In five years of teaching, he had nearly doubled his salary and reached into the secluded world of the graduate seminar. The overwhelming question in my mind became what happened in that fifth year that resulted in the seldom-used expedient of buying up a contract?

The answer was not in the papers, the bulk

of which were recommendation letters from the Department for contract renewal, his original résumé, with more recommendation letters in support of his application for a position in the Department, and various and sundry course proposals.

Apart from the fact that it was Saunsoci University that had granted him his Ph.D., the résumé revealed several other things that astounded me:

First of all, at the time of his initial appointment, he was only twenty-two years old, which meant that the broken, shredded creature in the crevice was now only thirty-nine years old.

Which, on reflection, should not have surprised me as much as it did, for who does not remember what happened to the great Artaud, the ghastly decay, wrought in nine short years of lucidity before he found a home in Van Gogh's eye and a "singing brother" in Van Gogh's heart?"

Secondly, at the time of his appointment, Shitmouth was married.

That rocked me back in the Dean's chair and set my head spinning.

Shitmouth married!

I could have imagined him in a thousand postures, confronting reality, and it would never have occurred to me to see him in a home with a wife and daily doings; shopping; mowing the lawn; eating at table; doing dishes; taking out the garbage; whispering intimacies in the darkness. It all exceeded the power of my imagination.

But there it was.

Bold print on the page.

"Married. No children."

Her name was Dawn.

I made a note of it and the address on the last

contract, a number on Saunsoci Lake, just outside the city.

The third thing I noted did not impress me much at the time, but it would cause me considerable wonder a year later. It was the place of his birth. A small town, two hundred miles from Saunsoci, on the horizon of the plains. A place called Thuddity. A year would pass before I learned that both Mary Hynes and Gabriel were also born and raised in that town, in the fields surrounding it.

The fourth piece of information that intrigued me was the subject of his Dissertation: "The Ontological Problematics of The Open; The Vast; and, The Eternal Return."

At the time, sitting there in the Dean's office, I could only think of tongue twisters and a mouth full of shit.

But I know better now.

I have read it a dozen times since Dawn gave it to me.

I have it here before me now.

It was his essay into "the crack between the worlds" which finally catapulted him into the center of the egg and the sorrow of all that is.

What staggers the imagination is how he ever got it accepted by a dissertation committee. He must either have embarrassed the hell out of them or charmed the pants off them. For, inspired by Nietzsche as it was, it destroyed academic philosophy in its very foundations and disclosed the creative foundations for the "transvaluation of all values," the foundations that the immortal Nietzsche never revealed.

However he managed to get it through, his

colleagues were to make sure that it never happened again.

And that was all the information the envelope had to offer.

I turned my attention to the tapes.

The first was dated from the second semester of his fourth year, after he had already received his final contract but a semester before it became effective.

I threaded the recorder.

Switched it on.

Tones of pompous officiality addressing the invisible.

The Dean was effecting a decision:

"Reports having reached this office of irregularities in the conduct of his seminars; to wit: speaking over the heads of his students; using vulgarity in the classroom and conducting a line of inquiry detrimental both to the integration of the Department and to the hallowed traditions in the history of philosophy, I am this day assigning Stephen Jorgensen to the classes of Dr. Robert Tanner. He will keep an eye on the situation and make the customary reports to me."

Stunned, I played it back.

And then again.

It was there like a bomb in the ear.

Stephen was a spy in Shitmouth's classes!

Suddenly, all the uneasiness, embarrassment, and shiftiness I had seen whenever I raised a question about Shitmouth's past became clear. Stephen knew that if I pursued that past, I would find out that he was a spy.

I shut the recorder off.

Swirled in the chair.

Stared out at the gauze of twilight forming over Saunsoci below until my mind went blank, and lights began to pop on in the city.

It finally occurred to me that Stephen knew I was here and might very well have called the police. Shivers went up my spine.

Quickly, I turned back to the tape deck.

"Now, Mr. Jorgensen," the Dean continued, "do you understand the assignment? You will enroll in Dr. Tanner's seminars, tape his lectures, and report anything else you may see or hear which does not seem to be in accordance with good academic practice."

"I understand."

"Good. This briefcase contains all the recording equipment you will need. It is locked. You are never to open it. Just set it on the table or desk, push the lock to the left to start it; to the right to stop it. Is that clear?"

"Yes, sir. Perfectly clear."

"Good. You're first report will be due a week from today. Do you have any questions whatsoever?"

Silence on the tape.

"You're worried if what you will be doing is legal?" the Dean asked.

"Well . . . yes. I've never done this before. I thought there might be a conflict with academic freedom or something."

"Yes, yes," the Dean replied, "I thought so. Beginners usually have those doubts. We like to think of them as rookies in that respect. But don't you worry, Mr. Jorgensen. The university and myself, especially, are very much dedicated to preserving and strengthening academic freedom. Dr. Tanner's colleagues have requested this investigation in order that they may have the freedom to continue to explore matters of serious thought with their students free of disruptive and negating influences. Never worry, Mr. Jorgensen. The University stands one hundred per cent behind its faculty. Yet it sometimes happens that a stranger gets into the community who does not cherish its values and makes all sorts of trouble for the others. Obviously, the academic freedom of that particular individual becomes inconsistent with the preservation of the freedom of the other members of the community. What we want to find out is whether or not Dr. Tanner is truly a member of our community. Do you see?

"Yes, sir. But I was also wondering if I would not be more effective and less suspicious if someone worked with me?"

"What do you have in mind?"

"My wife. If we joined the classes together, wouldn't it seem less suspicious in the long run?"

"Husband and wife entering the field of ideas together? Splendid, Mr. Jorgensen! Splendid! We've never used that approach before. I'll contact the Registrar and have the proper vouchers filed for her free tuition and the usual stipend. Now is there anything else?"

"No, sir."

"Fine. Then I'll see you in a week."

The tape ended.

Of the dozen or so tapes that followed, most were lectures. Apparently, the main body of the lectures for the semester had been edited to distill only the most damaging material.

The first was an introductory lecture on the history of philosophy, which opened with the statement:

"The history of philosophy is at an end as surely as both God and man are dead. If we are to grasp even the possibility of thought, we must understand radically, that is, we must journey to the source of thought in human beings and more especially to that human being yet to emerge, to be reborn. This was, of course, the overwhelming message of Nietzsche. In the course of this semester, we will see into the truth of that message and dump the history of philosophy on the shit pile where it belongs; where everything belongs that has raped human nature and walked away from human being."

Shitmouth was thundering.

His voice created echoes in the tape.

Various exclamations from the audience.

Then he proceeded to tie the history of philosophy into a ball and slam it off the wall of human existence; war and pestilence; violence and pillage and terror unremitting until he came to Rousseau.

"This fucker," he announced, "was as masochistic in thought as he was in bed, and the day came in history when the masochism of his thought found its sadistic partner. That, my friends, was Fascism, organically grown in the fields of Rousseau's masochism."

There followed a long reading from the prose of the poet Heine in which Shitmouth appeared to find the prophecy of Fascist Germany a hundred years before its dawn.

And so the tapes went.

I could not pretend to comprehend ninety percent of what they contained. Even the lecture titles left me dizzy. In the seminar on Aesthetics, for example, he called for a renewed and greatly expanded science of Hermeneutics. A call for, as he put it, "the liberation of this ancient and honorable science from the moldy but still brutal dungeons of corrupt theology and piss-ant theologians with trivial minds and pasty faces."

A comment that reminded me of Gabriel at the time.

The seminar on ontology was a breathless affair.

As quiet as the others were volatile.

The tapes were difficult to hear. Shitmouth seemed to be speaking in a whisper, most of the time in Greek and German and with constant reference to what he called "the immense prerevolutionary importance of Heidegger." It was as though, having burned the entire history of thought in the white heat of his mind, he was now turning and poking in the ash to see if something pure remained.

He spoke of the necessity of breaking Kant's back, from which he seemed to see issue all the errors of the modern comprehension and corruption of truth and reality.

He spoke for some time of Hegel's concept of "transparency," which he called the "deepest, most profound wonder of human thought and that which has never been understood."

Through Descartes and what seemed to be endless arguments with a student named Derek, he analyzed the relationship between narcissism and solipsism and concluded that "the id is full of light."

He said: "Everything changes if the id is full of light. There is your beginning."

As I listened to him speaking on the tapes, I lost all sense of time and place, and the slick executive decor of the dean's office melted into the grease of Harry's Bar, into the luminosity I had felt there as he talked, hunched over the broken table, and everything was as it has been forever, a man fighting to sustain the truth of his nature and the purity of his thought in the crazed realities of others who had long since fled from theirs.

Nothing made this clearer to me than the tapes involving the senior members of the department who had requested the investigation.

"I believe I speak for the rest of the department," the chairman said, "when I insist that this sort of thinking must not be allowed to continue."

"That is your conclusion after a careful consideration of the tapes?" the Dean asked.

"Yes, it is. My colleagues and I have observed a growing arrogance among our students, a trend toward individualistic thinking. They mock our objective examinations and attempt to embarrass our logic with pure Nietzschian rhetoric, and it is most disturbing to have our models, which we worked so hard to emulate the pure sciences with, challenged by what amounts to the ravings of a madman. It has, indeed, saddened the Department that Dr. Tanner is one of our own, and, quite frankly, we believe he has lost his mind and needs professional help."

"Have you spoken with him about this?"

"We have tried, but he laughs in our faces, and now he doesn't even attend our meetings."

"Doesn't attend your meetings!" the Dean boomed.

A murmur of affirmation from the group.

"But that is a requirement under his contract. All faculty must attend Departmental meetings unless they have an authorized excuse. Did he give you one?"

"Nothing acceptable," the Chairman replied.

"May I suggest," another voice intruded, "Dr. Greenberg, that you tell the Dean the details of our last meeting with Dr. Tanner."

Silence.

"Yes. By all means," the Dean said. "But I must have the minutes of the last faculty meeting right here somewhere."

Drawers banged on the tape.

"Yes. Here it is. I saw nothing out of the ordinary in it."

"I edited the minutes," the Chairman said. "We didn't want to disturb your office. We honestly thought we could bring Dr. Tanner into line."

"Do you mean to tell me, Dr. Greenberg, that you are forwarding false reports to my office?"

"False is a little strong, sir. I simply omitted an incident."

"Dr. Greenberg, in my long experience as an administrator, I have found that the worst trouble inevitably begins with omissions!"

"It won't happen again," the Chairman replied.

"And you had better be very certain of that!" the Dean shouted. "Now, explain the incident you referred to."

"It involved a Ph.D. candidate who has been working under Dr. Tanner, a Mr. Derek."

"Yes?"

"I called a Departmental meeting to consider the acceptability of his dissertation, and the majority of the Department agreed with me that the dissertation should not be allowed, but Dr. Tanner objected violently. He said . . ."

There was a pause on the tape and the sounds of uneasy movement.

"May I speak quite frankly, sir?" the sounds of uneasy movement.

"May I speak quite frankly, sir?" the Chairman asked.

"Yes. Yes, by all means."

"Dr. Tanner said that we were all a bunch of lily-livered assholes who couldn't recognize an original thought in a sea of turds."

"Dr. Greenberg!" the Dean exclaimed.

"I'm sorry, sir, but that is exactly what he said."

"He addressed the senior faculty members in such a manner?"

"Yes. And we were all quite saddened because he was one of our own. We see now, in retrospect, that we should never have allowed his own dissertation to pass, but we thought he would eventually transcend his youthful enthusiasms."

"Well, that's all water under the bridge now," the Dean said. "Why did the Department find this Mr. Derek's dissertation unacceptable?"

"It attempted to justify solipsism."

"Solipsism?"

"Solipsism."

"What in heaven's name is solipsism?" the Dean asked.

"Briefly," the Chairman replied, "it holds to the thesis that nothing is real apart from the individual's own experience. It is probably the oldest fallacy in the history of philosophy. All the great thinkers avoid it like the plague and warn against it because it leads directly to anarchism."

"Mr. Derek is supporting anarchism?"

"And Dr. Tanner with him."

"Well, I should think the Department showed a great deal of wisdom in rejecting such a thesis. Did you explain to Dr. Tanner that history would not bear him out?"

"We did."

"He said: 'Bullshit. History is dead and everybody knows it!' He claimed that Mr. Derek's dissertation was representative of something entirely new, and anarchism was a spook of the academic mind. Of course, we reminded him that the dissertation was representative of and responsible to the field and should reflect the concerns of the academic community, to say nothing of the university itself."

"And what was his response to that?"

"He got up and left with Mr. Derek."

"Mr. Derek was there all the time?"

"Yes, sir."

"When Dr. Tanner insulted the senior members of the Department?"

"Yes."

"Well, clearly, Dr. Tanner will have to be disciplined!" the Dean exclaimed.

"He said one other thing before he left," the

Chairman said quietly, "which is prejudicial to my authority and leadership in the Department."

"What is that?"

"He said, and I quote him exactly: 'The dissertation owes its allegiance to nothing but the creative advancement of thought. It's not a fucking bar mitzvah!' "

"Well, gentlemen," the Dean concluded, "I can see that Dr. Tanner is certainly not the kind of person we want teaching our students. Steps will be taken."

Steps were taken.

Goose steps, as always.

The last tape contained Shitmouth's interview with the Dean:

"Dr. Tanner," the tape began. "Your appointment was scheduled for two. It is now two-thirty."

"I know," Shitmouth replied. "I was thinking."

"Yes, indeed. And do you think that is the proper attitre for the academic community? It looks like a quilt to me."

"It is."

Shitmouth had apparently worn his quilt of many colors to his inquisition.

He said: "I fail to see where what I wear is any concern of yours. What did you call me here for?"

"Dr. Tanner, I am afraid I must ask for your resignation from the University."

Shitmouth laughed.

"This is not a laughing matter, Dr. Tanner! I must insist on your resignation immediately!"

"I have the better part of a three-year contract remaining."

"And I," the Dean replied, thumping the desk, "have enough material here to see that you are fired if you do not resign immediately."

"What have you got there?"

The Dean checked off the list from the use of obscenities in the classroom to insulting superiors in the presence of students.

"The fact is, Dr. Tanner, that your colleagues find your continuation here intolerable."

"How do you know what I'm saying in the classroom?" Shitmouth asked.

"That is none of your business, Dr. Tanner. Students have complained of your behavior."

"Who? Name one."

"No, Dr. Tanner. That is confidential information between the students and myself."

"You're a damn liar!" Shitmouth shouted. "You've placed spies in my classes and completely corrupted an educational process that was corrupt to the bone as it was."

"Dr. Tanner, I must remind you that I am the Dean!"

"You sure are," Shitmouth replied. "Now I'm going to tell you something, Dean. Not only am I not going to resign, but if you persist in your attempts to have me fired, I will take you directly to Court. There won't be any fucking around with the Academic Affairs Committee or the AAUP, which are as corrupt as you. I'll take you directly to Court for the violation of every known right of privacy and freedom of thought. Win or lose, it'll raise a stink that will see even your most conservative alumni returning their degrees."

The Dean was silent.

"My attorney will be in to see you in the

morning," Shitmouth said. "You can discuss with him the details of his investigation into your operation."

That was it.

So began the chain of events that concluded in the purchase of Shitmouth's contract "For the good of the University and academic community."

I returned everything to the file.

Replaced the key.

Left.

XIV

Evening classes were dismissing as I walked out the front of the building.

Hundreds of students trying to shake off the boredom they had just sustained. Their inane but colorful chatter danced with the lights of the city below.

But the warm breeze was sour on my face, and I became acutely depressed.

It wasn't until then that the appalling evil of the whole thing settled over me, and walking through the students, I felt deeply ashamed of what I knew, for they did, most certainly, come with books and the desire to learn. Men and women do dream of learning, a richly begotten dream rising out of the inertia of living and propelling the imagination toward peace, beauty, and the long thought.

And I knew they came to the wrong place, as they themselves would come to know and hide that dream away forever in their living. And I was ashamed of knowing that. The kind of shame that America's Homer, big Tom Wolfe found in himself; the thing he called "the dark wound of America" and the terrible shame and hurt that it entails in all who see it. To know that men and women dream the more perfect, the more fulfilling thing and, out of fear or indolence, layer it with scum and render the fresh fetid is a knowledge life can not support and becomes an abiding shame and the curse of all those who stand apart with conscience.

It occurred to me, as I walked down the hill into the city, that Shitmouth was soaked in that shame, and I felt quite close to him.

He was in the crevice.

Sleeping.

Drawn into the fetal position, his hands clasped together between his legs.

His body a torrent of shaking.

A nauseating stench, emanating from his coffee cans, filled the air.

I sat down at the corner of the building and fell into a reverie about his wife. What kind of a woman was she? Where was she now, and could I find her? Could I bring her here and hope she could hold this rotten mess in her arms and nurse it back to health and the certain step of a man?

I could not even begin to put a face on her.

Nor was there time.

Shitmouth started vomiting.

Unbelievable sounds.

It was as though he were trying to throw up his soul.

I crept into the crevice.

Removed a can of yellowish watery shit.

Yellow green bile spurted from his mouth into the other can.

Sweat poured from his face.

I sat down and held his head.

The convulsions lasted for several minutes.

Terrifying.

I felt as though I were holding death in my arms, and I trembled with fear.

I vaguely remember screaming: "Jesus Christ! Jesus Christ, it is enough!" And I wanted a hammer, anything to smash that egg and free him.

And I remember crying.

My eyes just simply exploded with tears, which was so strange to me because, as far back as I can remember, I had never really cried over another human being. Hatred had dried me up long, long ago.

Finally, the convulsions subsided, and he laid his head in my lap.

Wiping the sweat from his face and stroking his hair, I felt vaguely like a woman, but I couldn't begin to describe the feeling correctly. Something like reassurance. Something like protectiveness.

Something I sensed in my mother when she died rocking me to sleep in her arms.

Something like love.

He said: "Water."

The only thing I could find to put it in was a half-empty whiskey bottle. I dumped it out and ran to the fountain in front of the building.

Filled it.

He drank too much, of course, and the convulsions began all over again.

And so it went until my fear turned to anger and I realized that something had to be done.

I took the water away from him.

I said: "Shitmouth, I'm going to call an ambulance."

His hand gripped my leg like steel.

He said: "No! Just sleep. I need to sleep."

Fumbling in his rags, he came out with the medallion, and clutching it tightly in his fist, drew back into the fetal position.

In time, his body did seem to relax a little.

Looking up the wall of the crevice into the billion stars, I saw something I had not noticed before. The walls seemed to slant inward as they went up, forming the inside of a cone. And for a split second, I thought I saw a large bird perched at the top.

I said: "Shitmouth, I'm going to find your wife."

His eyes opened.

Froze mine with that terrible intensity he had.

As I moved to leave, he said: "Wait."

Fumbled in his rags again.

Came out with a small bankbook.

He said: "Give her this."

I said: "Do you know where she is?"

He did not answer.

Folded back into himself.

I did not open the book until I got to Harry's

Stephen and Gabriel were sitting in a booth drinking beer.

I put contempt in my face. Ordered a beer. Sat in Shitmouth's chair.

The bankbook began with a twenty-thousand-dollar deposit and ended with a twenty-thousand-dollar balance. It had been opened ten years before under both their names, and the interest had been withdrawn four times a year.

Another mystery dissolved.

Shitmouth did not make his money selling booze to the kids at school as I had always supposed. He lived off the interest from the money, which he must have gotten when they bought up his contract. And not too much of the interest, either, as I was later to find out. Most of it went to Gabriel and the funds that were being set aside to open the bookstore.

I checked the address on the bankbook against the one I had taken from his contract. It was the same number on the West Shore of Saunsoci Lake.

Absorbed, I did not see Stephen approach.

He leaned across the table.

He said: "So you found out."

"I found out. How come you didn't call the cops and tell 'em I was there?"

He shook his head. "There is a lot you don't know or understand yet, Shakey. Why don't you come over and have a beer with us?"

"I don't think I could stand the stink."

Anger flashed in his face.

117

His fist balled.

He said: "Then we'll join you. One way or the other, you're going to get the story straight."

"Suit yourself."

He waved Gabriel over.

I felt suddenly very old.

Very tired.

Drained.

"Diane and I did spy on him for a while," Stephen began. "But we didn't think of it as spying. The whole system is so bizarre and complex, we simply thought of it as a job, and if we hadn't done it, someone else would have. The whole affair would have turned into a bigger mess for him than it did, though it is hard to see how it could have turned out any worse for us."

"What do you mean?"

"Diane is in the nut house now as a direct result of our getting involved with Tanner."

"That's right," Gabriel assured me.

"And she'll never come out," Stephen continued. "She claims she's found enlightenment in there, and she's perfectly happy just sitting in a corner laughing her ass off all day."

"How did she get in?"

"I'm coming to that. Her parents threw her in. He's a rich-bitch surgeon, and now they couldn't get her out if they wanted to. She won't go."

In time, of course, after we took Mary's body home to Thuddity, Gabriel, Stephen, and I broke into the assylum to sit in the corner and listen to Diane's laughter.

No cackling there.

No giggling.

Her laughter seemed to come from the belly

of the universe, and it terrified me, like Shitmouth's vomiting.

Somehow, she had made the connection.

Found the turn.

Sat inside the egg with Shitmouth.

"You know the funny thing is, she turned against the spying thing before I did," Stephen continued. "These bastards are clever. They assign spies in areas where they have no interest. I was a Bus. Ad. major and Diane was in Phys. Ed., and we were just twenty and dead broke because her fucking parents didn't want us to get married and wouldn't give us any help. And Deirdre was coming. Now what the hell does a Bus. Ad. or a Phys. Ed. major know about philosophy? Hell, we couldn't even spell the word at the time. Then, one day, she walked out of one of those lectures on the primordial relationship between the body and the word, and she wouldn't speak to me for hours. I thought she was having her goddamn period or something."

"The same thing happened to me," Gabriel said. "Just all of a sudden, one day, there it is, and you realize that you're completely unprepared no matter how much you thought you understood."

"Exactly," Stephen said. "We were walking down by the river, and she turned around to me and said: 'You know we're a couple of dumb bastards. We're sitting right in the middle of a whole new world and can't even see it.' "

"The strength and breadth of it was far too vast to see," Gabriel said. "And it still is. Tanner was on the verge of stopping history and starting time all over again. I don't mean in any messianic or apocalyptic sense but just in terms of the radicalness of pure thought. But, in those days, it sounded like a foreign language, and we wasted all that time.

"Anyway," Stephen interrupted, "we went back and started listening, and it was good-by to Bus. Ad. and good-by to Phys. Ed. and it was good-by tape recorder. We took it out to his house and told him what they were doing and threw the fucking tape recorder in the lake and told him we would testify against them if they ever brought it up."

"What did he say," I asked.

"Little about that. Just laughed, more or less. I think he knew it would happen sooner or later. But you know something? I never met a man who loved this country with the depth and passion that he did. He talked for a long time about the sorrow of the world that is the true foundation of American reality and how, out of the knowledge of that sorrow, we could build a culture unlike anything ever seen in the history of man if we were only strong enough to get to the foundation and commence building from it."

I said: "I know. He told me about it in a different way, but, my God, it's hell."

"You're telling me," Stephen said. "But I think that afternoon at the lake was the first time I ever thought of being a poet, and how long is it now? Over ten years, and I haven't even begun."

"Weren't there any protests when they bought him out?"

"Sure, but he had gotten past the point of no return by then. He'd meet the classes and take them to a bar, or he'd roll in dead drunk and say there was no way he was talking to anybody because he was thinking, and thought didn't have a schedule. The finale came when he walked in naked one day with only the quilt over his shoulders. He said: 'I have a letter from France. There is a rumor that Merleau-Ponty has just broken through to ontology and set the foundation for our new beginnings. Get out of your fucking clothes, clear your minds, and listen to this: "The Flesh of the Body + The Flesh of the World = Being.' Diane had an orgasm on the spot. He said: 'Get inside the space of your body and think like you've never thought before and then answer me this: What words would follow such a formulation? What clear and unknown words could follow the beauty of this thing and what songs? What colors?' "

"What did they say?"

"Say?" Stephen laughed. "We sat there for three solid hours and couldn't say a fucking thing. Christ! If I could find just one such word, I could have my beginning."

"We could build a true religion from there," Gabriel murmured.

I couldn't see his weakness anymore. His limpid eyes no longer testified to weakness and adolescent awkwardness. They traveled inside like a mist on the heath and rested in a future yet to be.

"Protests?" Stephen said. "Yeah, Gabriel, Diane, and I organized protests, but Tanner only showed up once. That was the day they carted Diane away. She was sitting naked out in front of the administration building with the flesh of the body formula on a placard, and several hundred of us were sitting in front of her. All of us stark ass naked. Then Tanner came and sat down next to Diane and wrapped her in the quilt. And right on his heels came the cops and hustled her off."

"Did Shitmouth say anything?" I asked.

"I want to tell you he did," Stephen replied. "He turned against us, or so we thought at the time. He said there would be no protests in his name, that it was not his way. He said protests drain the energy from dreams and quiet building in secluded places. He said that if we wanted to protest something, we should go into hiding and protest against ourselves and the limitations of what we knew. He stood up with the quilt around his shoulders and cocked his ear at us. He said: 'I have not heard the words yet or the songs. Neither have I seen the colors. They are still entombed in darkness, and I protest against that, and I protest against you for leaving them there and fucking off like this. Teach yourselves.' And he walked off, and our vigor curdled into shame."

Gabriel said: "We didn't see him for five years after that."

"Then we started coming to the crevice," Stephen said. "But he wouldn't say anything to us anymore. He'd just sit and listen. He said it was time for us to teach him."

"Did you?"

"How could we? Derek is the only one who could ever follow the intricacy of his logic. The whole thing turned into a series of booze sessions, and we quit going after a while."

"Did Derek ever get his Ph.D.?" I asked.

"Hell, no! They threw him out of the Department as soon as they got rid of Tanner. He went up on a hill over the city one beautiful dawn when the leaves were turning and opened his veins. They brought him down at dusk. Dead. Said he wanted to merge with infinity and had found the freedom to do that."

"Well, that's the end of our part in the thing," Stephen said. "We would have told you sooner, but it's all a goddamn nightmare, and I don't like to think about it, especially the shit that fell on Diane. It hurts too much."

"You see," Gabriel said, "the future is now our past."

I didn't see at all.

Not for a long time to come.

"Yeah," Stephen said. "Let's go home."

"You mean I can still stay with you?"

"Why not?"

Back at the room, Candy was sleeping on Stephen's mattress.

Deirdre on mine.

And that is the way it would remain.

Before I fell asleep, I said: "Stephen, I'm going to talk to Shitmouth's wife."

"Yeah," he replied. "Better take some sunglasses along."

"Why?"

"Her beauty will shock your eyes."

XV

And so it did.

Saunsoci Lake was one of the few lakes in the country that had not been turned into a cesspool, thanks to the foresight of wealth.

Seven miles long and a little over a mile wide, its banks were lined with the summer homes of the rich, and the shores were decorated with their various craft, boathouses, and docks.

It was yet early in the morning when I made my way there. The sun glistened on the still water, deep blue in the center, clear green at the shores. A warm breeze slightly stirred the air.

Coming from the ghetto, the lake both intimated me and roused a vague sense of freedom which, when joined, turned into a kind of paranoia. I found myself expecting some authority to challenge my presence there.

But the bankbook in my pocket bathed me in security.

I had a mission.

In time, I found the address.

From the road, a long rolling yard flowed down to a reddish-brown ranch house that must have run to forty or fifty thousand dollars.

The back of the house faced the road, the front circled by a sun deck that opened on the lake and the white-sand beach. A foreign sports car was in the drive.

The mailbox bore the stencil: "R. Tanner."

I was relieved that she still lived there.

Slowly, I made my way down the drive to the sun deck, where I had caught a slight movement out of the corner of my eye.

Even now, as I sit here in the fullness of memory and know all the things that happened between us and continue to happen, I am still stunned by the images of that morning.

Women had always made me feel shy, even the hardest of the ghetto women, with their sour faces and cruel mouths and their screaming and hollering. But Dawn made me feel immensely shy.

Painfully shy.

She stood at the railing looking out over the

lake, her long amber hair floating gently down her back, briefly stirred by the breeze. The blue and white chiffon peignoir she was wearing parted and closed, revealing long, tanned legs.

At first, I could not see her face, and overwhelmed by the grace that confronted me, I stopped short and did not move.

I could sense that my mouth was hanging open, but I did not know how to close it.

For some time, she stood sensing the sun, the water, and the breeze, and when she did turn, there were tears on her cheeks.

I don't think she saw me for a moment or so.

Her face was deeply tanned and classically long, her eyes as blue as the center of the lake.

It would have thrilled a film to cast and contain her.

When she did speak, it was harshly: "Who the hell are you? What are you doing here?"

I could see she was alarmed.

I fumbled with my mouth.

"Well! I'm waiting!"

I said: "Mrs. Tanner?"

"Yes."

"I came to talk to you about your husband."

"Is he dead?"

"No."

"Too bad."

Her face became a scowl.

"Well, are you just going to stand there? Come up and sit down."

I mounted to the sun deck, which was furnished with yellow cushioned lawn chairs, a wrought-iron glass-topped table, and a yellow umbrella.

The front of the house was a maze of glass sliding doors.

I tried to get an image of Shitmouth living in the place.

But I failed.

Sitting down, I found I could see through Dawn's robe.

She wore nothing under it, and I was extremely embarrassed and embarrassed further about being embarrassed.

One does not come easily into the presence of the perfect naked body, which moves with grace and understanding and in so doing banishes despair and nothingness.

"If he's not dead, what do you want to talk to me about?" she asked, stretching out on the chaise, her robe falling away from her legs and trailing down to the floor.

I averted my eyes.

Stared out over the lake.

I said: "I want to know how you lived and what happened to him the last few years at the University. And I think I want to take you to him because he is very sick."

"Not on your life," she replied. "I've already spent my time in hell with his sickness. I haven't seen him in eight years, and I don't care if I ever see him again. Say, what are you, anyway? A reporter? Because if you are, you're not getting anything out of me unless you pay for it. The bastard left me with nothing."

"No, I'm not a reporter, and I don't have any money. I hitched out here."

"You one of his flaky students? But how could you be? He hasn't done anything in ten years, and you don't look a day over twenty. How old are you?"

"Twenty."

"How do you know him?"

"I met him on the streets."

"Falling down drunk, I suppose."

"Yes."

"The bastard," she said bitterly.

I said: "He's been teaching in the City of Light."

"Oh, my God!" she exclaimed. "I think I'm going to be sick! He's got your head twisted up with that crap, too, has he?"

"I don't understand."

"That figures. Neither did the rest of them, and he ruined their lives just like he did mine."

She gathered her robe over her legs and glowered at the lake.

A bomb set to explode.

"The City of Light!" she spat. "What a load of shit!"

She flung herself out of the chaise.

I thought she was going to hit me.

Ducked.

"I need a drink," she snapped.

Disappeared into the maze of glass.

I was as alarmed by her violence as I had been by her beauty.

She could be vicious.

I brought out the bankbook and laid it on the table between us.

She returned with a gin and tonic.

Stood at the railing for a few moments, her face on the water. Then turned. Scowled at me.

"I think you better leave," she said quietly.

"I've heard all this before, and I don't need the torment of remembering it."

I picked up the bankbook.

Handed it to her.

She said: "What's this?"

"He said I should give it to you."

She leafed through it.

She said: "So the bastard's been holding out on me all these years!"

Then her expression changed.

Softened.

"When did he give you this?"

"Last night."

"And you say he was sick?"

"I didn't think he was going to make it. The vomiting wouldn't stop."

She winced.

Turned away.

"I remember the vomiting," she said hoarsely. "It was all over the place. He couldn't go anywhere without a bucket. My God, you'd think he'd have learned by now."

I said: "The medallion seemed to have calmed him."

"The medallion." She sighed. "That lousy medallion was the start of all the trouble. Days on end without a word; just sitting and toying with that damn medallion. And that filthy quilt he carted home one day. I should have burned it the first time I saw it! Does he still have the quilt?"

"No. Do you remember where he got it?"

"He told me he got it in an old bookstore in town, but I don't know."

"And the medallion?"

"Probably got that from one of his girl friends!

He told me he got it out of an egg. Imagine that!"

"He was seeing someone else?"

"He was screwing his students is what he was doing."

"How do you know?"

"I caught him with one of them one day going at it a mile a minute under that damn quilt in the study. I should remember her name. Her goof of a husband was sitting right there watching them and tried to get me out of the room. Yes . . . Diane something or other."

"Jorgensen?"

"Yes, that's it. Do you know her?"

"No. I know her husband and their little girl. Diane's been in the nut house for years."

"Probably where she belongs," Dawn quipped. "It wouldn't have been so bad, I suppose, but he would never make love to me after he brought that quilt home; wouldn't even sleep in my bed again."

Her fists clenched around the glass.

"Said if I wanted to make love, it would have to be under the quilt where he had been screwing all the others."

I said: "He wanted to take you to the City of Light."

Her lower lip trembled.

"He promised he would take care of me," she said simply.

And how long would I live and wonder over what that meant in the voice of a woman?

Long.

Far too long.

To learn that to care is to set free within the orbit of intimacy and the daily gaze that will not be broken by reality.

Learning that we are never prepared for in the bunch and thrust of living.

Thus it was that sitting there on the sun deck that morning, I did not know:

Had no way of knowing.

That, in Dawn's simple phrase, was the truth of the breeze I had been seeking from Shitmouth.

She said: "What do you do?"

"I write plays."

Doubt flickered in her eyes.

I said: "I've already had one produced by the Community Play House."

She said: "There was a play a few years ago. A strange little thing I couldn't understand. It was suppose to be written by a young boy. Something about the sun?"

"Yes."

"That was yours?"

"Yes."

"I couldn't understand it. There weren't any people in it."

"You were in it, but they cut that part out."

It wasn't until I said it that I knew it was true. Dawn was the dream of the sun that I always knew was there and had longed to waken.

"Me?" she said. "I've never seen you before. How could I have been in your play?"

"I don't know. But you were there at the very end. The sun was playing with your body, asking you to wake."

Her gaze moved out over the water, and the breeze thickened with the showering of the sun.

She said: "That is what it was like when we were first married; when we first came here. Waking with the sun. Playing with love. Enjoying life."

131

"How did you manage to keep this place going?"

"I work."

"I can't imagine you working."

She said: "I free-lance. I'm a landscape architect."

Her attention shifted from the water.

Fixed on me.

She said: "There's something about you that reminds me of him. Maybe it's the smell. When's the last time you had a bath?"

I remember feeling like a rat in paradise.

I said: "I'll leave."

"Don't you want to see his things?"

"Things?"

"Yes. His books and manuscripts."

"Sure."

"You'll have to take a shower first. You're not going to drag that smell through my house. There's a shower in the basement you can use."

The basement was tiled and paneled.

A fireplace.

A white bearskin rug.

A bar.

And a kimono hung for me.

A kimono of many colors.

Dawn was waiting for me as I stepped from the shower and wrapped myself in the kimono.

Upstairs, the house was a blur of luxury.

We stopped at the study door while she fumbled for a key.

I said: "You keep it locked?"

"I always thought he would come home someday, and we could begin all over again."

She said: "But you came instead."

The study was dark.

Musty.

She opened the drapes, and the sun shot into the room.

Then, she slid open the doors leading out on to the sun deck.

The breeze from the water joined the sun in the room, and the place was transformed into a miracle of dark wood and leather-covered books, as rich to the eye as the thoughts they contained were to the mind.

There was the feeling of rice paper and parchment in my hands, and my head swirled with fragmentary dreams of everlasting knowledge.

And standing there in the deep, Indian-green carpet in my bare feet, I could not move.

Dawn smiled.

Took my hand.

Led me to the massive ebony desk and set me down in a black, high-backed leather chair.

She said: "This is where he worked."

Quietly, she moved through the sun in the room, placing manuscripts before me.

They were Shitmouth's books and journals, which were never published, and when she set them before me, I could feel immense love in her hands.

"I had these bindings made in Spain," she said.

I felt the holy in the ring of her voice.

Felt fused with all that is holy among people.

And, as I had the night before, while holding Shitmouth's head in my hands, I exploded with tears.

But I was not afraid.

Dawn held my face.

Wiped it with her robe.

"Maybe it will not all be a waste," she said, "if you can understand something in these pages and teach it to me."

Then she left, closing the door to the study behind her.

And there before me, wrapped in soft Spanish leather, was the wonder of history yet to become a past.

The future.

Among whose pages I have felt honored to dream.

Opening them, I lost the sun in their titles. There was his dissertation: "The Ontological Problematics, of the Open; the Vast; and the Eternal Return."

And another, titled simply: *Behind the World.*

A third: *Inside the Cosmic Egg.*

And two that were unfinished and bound together: *Mind Beyond Time* and *The City of Light.*

It would be years before I understood them, and I knew it as I leafed through them.

I turned to the journals, thinking I could find more of his own history.

By the time I finished reading, I found the breeze had slipped away, and emeralds were embarrassed by the depths of the stillness which had settled into the lake.

Dusk was coming.

And the only relevant line I had found in the journals was simply this: "Drunkennesss hardens romanticism; curdles it with shame and despair. That is its health."

Dawn, dressed in white, said: "I'll drive you back to town."

In the car, she said: "You'll come back?"

"Yes."

I directed her to the crevice.

I said: "I'll show you where he lives."

She hesitated.

But her curiosity prevailed.

Shitmouth was not there.

But the incredible stench still emanated from the coffee cans.

It seemed not to affect Dawn.

She took off her shoes.

Slipped by me.

I could feel her eyes.

Blue.

Luminous.

Moving in the crevice.

I thought I heard her say: "I'm sorry. I'm sorry, my love."

I said: "He's probably at the bar."

She touched the ground inside the crevice.

Turned away.

On the way to Harry's, she said: "I wish I could have taught him about the body. About my body."

At the bar:

Shitmouth was at his table.

The old winos slumped like grease against the walls.

Shock when she entered.

The grease slipped down the walls.

Slid up on feet that contained no strength.

Wobbly-legged, they stood like puppets, watching our entrance with open mouths and startled eyes.

It was the first time I had ever seen them react in unison.

I could only imagine that inside their broken faces they were seeing some long-forgotten childhood image. Some long-forgotten promise.

I had the eerie sensation that we were moving in slow motion toward the back of the bar where Shitmouth, too, was struggling to his feet.

He looked not much better than I had seen him last night.

Still shaking violently.

Sweat trickling from his hair, down his face.

We stopped in front of the table.

Dawn looked at me quizzically.

I nodded.

"Robert," she whispered. "Robert, is that you?"

"Yes."

Then, reality fell apart.

She screamed.

Turned and slapped me hard.

Babbled in my face: "How could you do this to me! How could you do this to me?"

Then, she slapped me again.

"So this is your City of Light!" she screamed.

And fled the bar.

The winos slid back to the floor.

Dazed, I sat down at the table with Shitmouth.

When I could find my tongue, I said:

"Shitmouth was it really worth it to leave all that beauty behind, to waste it for this?"

He silenced me with a weary wave.

"You have seen enough to know a better question," he said.

Then he hunched over the table and grabbed my arm in a steel grip.

"It is precisely because so much beauty is there

that it must be conserved. It must find a place to endure forever."

A hellish scream tore across the room.

An old wino, who had been slumped against the toilet bowl, struggled to his feet. Screamed again.

He raised his arms over his head.

A knife flashed in his hands.

Tottered toward us.

As they had done when Dawn entered, the rest of the winos found their way to their feet.

Slowly, they shuffled around the one with the knife.

Strange, gurgling noises rose from their throats that, the closer they got to our table, took on the aspect of a primordial song; a chant.

They swayed like decaying drones at a birth or a death.

The one with the knife stopped in front of Shitmouth.

I thought he was going to kill him.

Reached out to stop the plunge.

Shitmouth grabbed my arm again.

Bent it back on the table.

The medallion was in his hand.

He held it in front of the old wino's eyes.

One more soul-searing scream, and the old wino plunged the knife into his heart and collapsed in Shitmouth's arms.

Shitmouth closed his eyes with the medallion.

Kissed them.

Nodded.

Slowly, the rest of them gathered the old wino in their arms.

Still gurgling their strange chant, they hoisted

his body to their shoulders and moved to the back entrance.

There was the crash of cans as they dumped his body in the alley.

Slowly, silently, they shuffled back to their places in the bar.

"Four screams a night is all you assholes get in here!" Harry shouted from the kitchen. "And I already heard four."

I said: "Shitmouth, what happened?"

He stared at me coldly.

Contemptuously, I thought.

I felt very small.

Irrelevant.

"A simple thing," he mumbled. "A warrior ripped the hymen of the cosmic mind, and his blood flowed on to the everlasting."

Then he closed his eyes.

Shuddered.

Slept.

I had the feeling I would never learn anything more from him, and I was swept with depression.

Stephen was up when I returned to the room.

Candy and Deirdre, asleep.

"Well?" he asked.

"You were right. I should have taken sunglasses."

He chuckled.

Before I fell asleep, I said: "Stephen, what did you learn when Shitmouth was fucking Diane?"

"She told you about that?"

"Yeah."

He was silent for a few minutes.

"Laughter," he said at last. "I heard the same laughter under the quilt that I hear from Diane in nut house."

XVI

In the morning, I gathered together my play about the wind.

Threaded my way through the ghetto.

A red beret stopped me.

He said: "The soul of the hawk flies in your face."

I said: "I know of the hawk."

He said: "Then I must tell you to beware today."

"Why?"

"Because my brothers and my sons are riding the strong winds on mighty horses, and they will bring the hawk out of the sky and purify the ash."

I said: "You mean it is time?"

"It is time."

"Then I will beware."

On out of the ghetto then.

Hitched to the lake.

Dawn was stretched out on the chaise on the sun deck.

Her face on the water.

I sat down beside her.

It was some time before she acknowledged my presence.

When she did, she said: "That was a terrible thing you did to me last night."

I said: "I'm sorry. I thought you wanted to see him. I thought it was natural."

"You said he was teaching in the City of Light."

"He is."

"Not that I can see. I've never seen such a sordid mess."

"You weren't looking."

She looked at me. Defiantly.

"If there's going to be any City of Light, let it be here on his earth where I can feel its ground under my feet and its breath in my body. I see in ways you could never think of seeing. I see in the warmth of intimacy what you think you see with abstraction."

I didn't understand what she was saying.

Or why she seemed so vehement about it.

I thought of telling her that Mary was a

woman and Candy, too, and that they both had gone. But, I decided not to push my luck. There was still far too much about the City that I did not know.

"I'm going for a swim," she said. "Did you come to study?"

"Yes."

"Well, don't forget to take a shower before you go in."

Clad in my kimono, I found the study door open.

Full of sun and breeze.

And a vase of fresh yellow flowers.

Before settling at the ebony desk, I walked down to the beach and squatted in the white sand.

Watched her swim.

She wore no suit.

Her bronze body floated like an October leaf, golden on the blue ripples of the sun-sparkled water.

And when she did stroke, it was with lean motions, leaving no wake.

She was made for water.

She was the water.

Fons et origo.

I felt my eyes dancing in my head and turned away to the study and the soft Spanish leather of the manuscripts unknown to the world until . . . until . . .

In time, Dawn came to the study.

Sat on the black leather couch and dried her hair.

Her robe falling away.

Unconcerned.

Finally, she said: "Make love to me."

Our eyes moved with each other.

And I closed my eyes and listened in her body.

Heard the song of the crevice and the song of Candy, and I listened.

And, far out on the edge of the song, I saw the City sitting like a child's toy in the lap of the sun.

And, I knew.

I knew.

And I whispered in her ear: "My God, it is all the same. It is all the same thing forever."

When we woke, she said: "What do you want most to do?"

I said: "I want to work here. I want to come here and finish my play about the wind."

"Why?"

"Today I found the truth of the breeze."

She said: "I'll drive you back to town."

Even from such a distance, we could see that Saunsoci was burning to the ground in its center.

I said: "Drop me at the edge of town and go home."

She said: "I am frightened."

I said: "It's as it should be. The Indians have returned to purify the ash."

She said: "You will come back?"

She said: "You can write your play with me."

"I'll come."

XVII

But it was late.

I skirted the ring of sirens and frightened faces.

Headed deep into the ghetto, choking on the thick smoke.

I had to talk to Shitmouth.

Had to tell him that he could go home now.

Had to tell him that all he sought and taught was there in the belly of Dawn.

The school was a volcano of fire and molten granite.

On crazy legs, I ran to Harry's.

The table at the back was smashed to kindling.

The winos were all gone.

I ran back to the school.

Hundreds of winos huddled outside the barricades and waited.

I waited with them.

When the authorities left, and only wisps of smoke remained, we moved forward.

The coffee cans were melted.

There was nothing but a mound of ash.

And full-throated laughter rising from the earth beneath.

And the medallion sitting in the center.

We sat through the night.

All of us.

And listened to the laughter.

Listened.

Until the sun smiled and the laughter died.

Then, I reached for the medallion.

The old winos nodded and began their garbled chant.

I scooped the ashes into my pocket and took them to Mary.

When I handed her the medallion, she said: "No. It is yours now."

Poured a tumbler of whiskey.

Dropped the ashes in.

Drank.

She said: "He will travel home with me."

XVIII

This remains:
    When I told Dawn of his death, she said:
"No. No, he's not dead. He's come back to me.
New and young."
    Taking away my kimono of many colors, she
said:
    "Come to my City. Come now."
    I did.

XIX

And the breeze moved on . . .